...ad with a glass of in hand."

—Shelf Awareness, starred review

"A fun and informative take on the cozy crime mystery, French style."

—Eurocrime

"It is easy to see why this series has a following. The descriptive language is captivating... crackling, interesting dialogue and persona."

—ForeWord Reviews

"The authors of the Winemaker Detective series hit that mark each and every time."

—Student of Opinions

"Francophiles, history buffs, mystery fans, oenophiles will want to add the entire series to their reading shelf."

—The Discerning Reader

"Intrigue and plenty of good eating and drinking... will whet appetites of fans of both *Iron Chef* and *Murder, She Wrote*."

—Booklist

"Another clever and highly entertaining mystery by an incredibly creative writing duo, never disappointing, always marvelously atypical."

—*Unshelfish*

"One of my favourite series to turn to when I'm looking for something cozy and fun!"

—*Back to Books*

"Wine lovers and book lovers, for a perfect break in the shadows of your garden or under the sun on the beach, get a glass of wine, and enjoy this cozy mystery. Even your gray cells will enjoy!"

—*Library Cat*

"Recommended for those who like the journey, with good food and wine, as much as tthe destination."

—*Writing About Books*

"The reader is given a fascinating look into the goings on in the place the story is set and at the people who live there, not to mention all the wonderful food and drinks."

—*The Book Girl's Book Blog*

"A quick, entertaining read. It reminds me a bit of a good old English Murder Mystery such as anything by Agatha Christie."

—*New Paper Adventures*

Late Harvest Havoc

A Winemaker Detective Mystery

Jean-Pierre Alaux
and
Noël Balen

Translated by Sally Pane

LE FRENCH BOOK ▌

First published in France as
Vengeances tardives en Alsace
by Jean-Pierre Alaux and Noël Balen

World copyright ©Librairie Arthème Fayard, 2005

English adaptation copyright ©2015 Sally Pane

First published in English in 2015
By Le French Book, Inc., New York

www.lefrenchbook.com

Translator: Sally Pane
Translation editor: Amy Richard
Proofreader: Chris Gage
Cover designer: Jeroen ten Berge

ISBN:
Trade paperback: 9781939474599
E-book: 9781939474605
Hardback (library edition): 9781939474612

*The intoxicating joy
of revenge fulfilled.*

—Honoré de Balzac

1

In just minutes, death would strike again.

The wax-colored skeleton, brandishing a heavy scythe in his left hand, would hit the bronze carillon with the ivory femur in his other hand: one clean hard stroke for each hour that had passed.

Renowned wine expert Benjamin Cooker was waiting, oblivious to the crowd gathering around him. But when the Bavarian tourists began elbowing and pushing him, he could no longer enjoy the moment. He stepped away from the enraptured spectators, who were cooing at the pudgy cherubs, one of them holding a bell and the other holding a sand clock, and oohing and aahing over the intricately carved cabinet, the Latin inscriptions, and the midnight-blue and gold face of the astronomical clock in the Cathedral of Our Lady of Strasbourg.

Benjamin took refuge at the Pillar of Angels to the right of the gigantic clock. He leaned against it. The coolness of the stone sent a shiver down his spine, and for some odd reason he thought of Virgile, his assistant. Where was he? Already flirting with some pretty young tourist at the back of the cathedral, no doubt. Oh well, he'd show up. Benjamin turned his attention to the tour guide.

"This was one of the seven wonders of Germany when Alsace-Lorraine was still German territory," the guide said before putting a finger to his lips to shush a pair of noisy visitors. The hand of the clock was about to reach twelve.

Death, laughing in the face of time, banged out the twelve strokes of noon, setting off the automata. One by one, the twelve apostles appeared and processed in front of Jesus: Simon, who was called Peter; Andrew, Peter's brother; James; John; Philip; Bartholomew; Thomas; Matthew, the tax collector; James, Thaddaeus; Simon; and Judas Iscariot.

A rooster at the highest point of the cabinet crowed and flapped its wings three times during this processional march, and Benjamin recalled Peter's renouncement of Jesus. "Before the rooster crows twice, you yourself will disown me three times," Jesus had told Peter the night before his crucifixion. The maker of this theatrical time-piece had been well versed in the Holy Scriptures.

Another group had gathered near the throng of Germans. They were elderly, and from what he could hear, Benjamin surmised they were members of a club from Provence.

"Mother of God!" one of them exclaimed each time a new figure appeared in the allegorical theater.

Benjamin heard them call their guide by name: Jeanne. She had silver hair and laughing eyes and clearly knew all about this cathedral and its timepiece. Her talk was peppered with intriguing and amusing anecdotes. He perked an ear and bristled when a few club members snickered at her German-like Alsatian accent.

"Legend has it that when this clock was completed, the astronomer who devoted his life to devising and building it had his eyes gouged out on the order of the city's magistrate."

"Why?" a woman asked, holding her purse close to her chest.

Jeanne narrowed her eyes and said quietly, "So that the artist could not reproduce such a work of art anywhere else."

"Did he die?" the purse clutcher asked.

"You'll notice that I said 'legend has it.' Not all legends are true," the guide said, inspecting Benjamin, who had surreptitiously infiltrated her group. "You, sir—you look like an educated man. Do you know if they really gouged out the eyes of the genius who created this clock?"

Benjamin felt the suspicious stares of the Provençal group, which did not recognize him as one of their own. Jeanne, however, took him by the arm as if to make him a privileged witness to the rest of her talk.

"So, my good fellow, tell me what you think."

"Um, to tell the truth, I have no informed opinion," Benjamin stammered.

Jeanne pushed her glasses to the bridge of her aquiline nose, lifted her chin, and began pontificating.

"As a matter of fact, the astronomer was much too old by then to recreate such a work. He soon became deaf and was unable to hear the ticking of this mechanism created for the glory of God. He descended into madness and lost all sense of time."

"Really?" Benjamin asked.

"Do you doubt my word, sir?" She looked him in the eye and smiled.

"All gifted storytellers embellish their accounts from time to time, and some even fabricate tales. Wouldn't you agree?" the winemaker said, holding her gaze.

"You force me to tell the truth," the guide conceded, clearly delighted that her presentation had struck a responsive chord with this elegant man in a Loden. "So pay close attention, Mr.... What was your name?"

"Benjamin."

"As in Benjamin Franklin?"

"That's exactly right. As far as I'm concerned, this clock is as much an enigma as the lightning rod."

"Mr. Benjamin, I love your sense of humor."

"You are quite witty yourself, Madam," Benjamin replied with a smile. Then he removed his arm from hers. Enough flirting, he thought.

By now, some members of the club were whispering and sniggering. Obviously, they weren't amused by the diversion. Jeanne raised her voice and resumed her talk, addressing the entire group while still keeping her eye on Benjamin, who was so unlike the seniors she was leading through the cathedral.

From that point on, she punctuated each well-substantiated point with a question.

"Isn't that so?" she'd ask, looking at the winemaker.

"Actually, this is the third clock in the Strasbourg cathedral. The first was built in the fourteenth century, and we don't know who created it. Parts of it are now in the city's Oeuvre Museum of Decorative Arts. It was called the Three Kings Clock. The second one was built in the sixteenth century. When it stopped working in 1843, it was replaced by the clock you see here. Now, can anyone tell me who built this third clock?"

Jeanne drew out the suspense and inched closer to Benjamin, who stood stock still, his hands behind his back.

"A boy happened to visit this cathedral and was upset that the beautiful clock was broken. He asked one of the cathedral guards why it wasn't working, and the guard told him that no one in the country had the expertise to repair it. With that, the boy declared that he would be that man. His name was Jean-Baptiste Schwilgué. Fifty years after he vowed to repair the clock he finally got his opportunity. By this time he was versed in clock making, mathematics, and mechanics. In fact, he went on to invent the adding machine. Building this clock took four years and thirty workers."

"Is that all?" the winemaker asked.

"Yes, Mr. Benjamin. By the looks of it, this clock would have required far more time and many more workers. But Schwilgué was a genius. He had spent his entire life studying the astronomical clock. He even dreamed of making one with a glass cabinet that would allow everyone to see the mechanisms inside. But the city deemed the project too costly. Imagine the gem we would have today if he had been given free rein."

"Yes, but even as it is, this is a true jewel," Benjamin said.

"Indeed, it is," the Alsatian woman agreed, giving the winemaker a warm smile.

At the end of the tour, Benjamin thanked Jeanne and tried to slip a bill into her hand. She refused it and instead handed him her business card.

"Our cathedral has thousands of treasures," she whispered in his ear. "I would love to show you all of them—the heraldic sculptures, the three Last Judgment paintings, and, of course, the celestial globe studded with five thousand stars. You must see it! Let's make a date to meet another day. Shall we?"

"I'm too intimidated by this clock to give you a date, much less a precise time. Let's leave it to providence…"

Benjamin hoped she would get the message. But instead of saying good-bye, she took his wrist and clung to it for a few seconds. The winemaker was silent. Finally, she let go and turned around to rejoin her tour group. Benjamin felt a twinge of guilt—was it because he had turned the woman down or because he had actually considered making that date with her? No, what he felt was pity for the guide. He was blessed with his wife, Elisabeth, whose intelligence and wit were beyond match.

Benjamin decided to look for Virgile and spotted his assistant ducking into a confessional to answer his cell phone. He'd have a word with him about that. But before he could give the reprimand a second thought, screams rose from the group gathered near the clock.

"Oh my God," someone shouted. "Get help, quick!"

"It's too late," a bald man said.

The winemaker retraced his steps and with some difficulty made his way through the crowd gathered around a small figure on the floor. Above the bloody forehead, he could see a mass of silver hair. Beside the body lay a pair of gold-framed glasses with broken lenses—Jeanne's glasses.

"What happened?" he asked.

"All of the sudden she just clutched her chest and dropped. She hit her head in the fall."

From his vantage point on the clock, the Grim Reaper attended the scene, a satisfied smile carved on his jaw. He waved his femur and struck the bell. It was exactly one o'clock in the afternoon.

When Benjamin Cooker pulled open the door of the centuries-old confessional, Virgile, as he suspected, was still on his device, cooing sweet nothings in the dark to a faraway lover.

Benjamin gestured toward the door, indicating he would wait outside. He made his way to the square in front of the cathedral. The holidays were approaching, and soon wooden chalets would fill this space and spill onto the neighboring side streets—they had since 1570. This was the site of France's largest and oldest Christmas market. Benjamin smiled at memories of strudel, wooden toys that delighted his daughter, Margaux, when she was young, and spices filling the air.

2

The Kammerzell House, where Benjamin and Virgile were dining, was one of Strasbourg's architectural splendors. It had been converted from a pub to a fine restaurant at the end of the nineteenth century, and recently a hotel had been added. Over the course of six centuries, thousands of patrons, both little-known and celebrated, had climbed the spiral staircase connecting the five floors of this food-lovers' temple. It was said that Guttenberg, Goethe, and Mozart had frequently eaten here. Now it was the winemaker's turn.

Benjamin, whose trek up the stairs had left him panting and feeling heavy, surveyed his surroundings. He admired the woodwork, the bottle-glass windows throwing iridescent colors on the white table linens, and the frescoes signed by Léo Schnug, an Alsatian painter known for his ruddy faces and naughty scenes seemingly right out of Boccaccio's *Decameron*.

Once they were seated, the maître d' was on guard. No wonder. Benjamin was examining the wine list and menu and pointing out the estab-lishment's specialties as if he were already quite familiar with them. His serious-diner look could make any headwaiter jumpy, even one at such a legendary restaurant. His tailored British jacket and Virgile's casually classy attire—gray slacks, ash-rose shirt, and light-gray blazer—would only amplify the mistrust. The man probably suspected that he was a critic for an important food and wine guide—like the *Cooker Guide*! No matter. Benjamin had a way of making friends sooner or later with a good restaurant's staff. For him, dining was an experience to be savored from start to finish.

"I'll begin with the *foie gras de canard* in gewürztraminer aspic. What about you, Virgile?"

"A dozen *escargots Kocher*—"

"Kochersberg," Benjamin clarified. "That's an excellent choice."

Ever since they had arrived in Alsace, Virgile had been mangling Alsatian words—for fun. He even suggested they were invented solely for the purpose of winning points in Scrabble.

"And next, may I suggest—"

Benjamin undermined the maître d's obsequiousness by immediately choosing a *cuissot de porcelet rôti aux épices douces*.

"Ah, our delicately spiced suckling pig is a fine choice. It's precisely the dish that I—"

"Excellent." The winemaker grinned at the waiter, pretending to be pleased that they had the same selection in mind. Virgile, meanwhile, was still trying to decide between beef tartar and the three-fish sauerkraut.

"That is the house specialty," the maître d said.

"Let's honor Alsace. Right, boss?"

"Absolutely," Benjamin said with a nod. "Provided, of course, that the three fish were caught in the River Ill or, failing that, in the Rhine."

"Alas, sir, I cannot guarantee that. May I leave you in the hands of our sommelier, who will guide you in—"

"That won't be necessary," Benjamin interrupted. He ordered a Frédéric Mallo grand cru Rosacker *vieilles vignes*. "A two thousand five, if you please."

"Very good, sir."

"And water for you, Virgile? You must be very thirsty, even penitential, after your lengthy conversation in the confessional today."

"Don't blame me, boss. If you remember, I answered the call. I wasn't making it. Before I left Bordeaux, I met this German chick who was harvesting grapes in Beauséjour Bécot. I was just helping her out, and now she won't stop calling."

"Right. You were just helping her out. Whatever you say."

"She's a real babe, but—"

"How you talk about women, boy. You met some chick who's a babe? Come now, Virgile.

You have a refined palate, and you love wines with great subtlety, and yet you talk like a stable boy who tumbles in the hay with anything in a skirt."

"Boss! You don't give me enough credit."

"Well, then, prove me wrong."

As the winemaker and his assistant waited for their dishes to arrive, the pale yellow riesling with green reflections was awakening their senses. Benjamin changed the subject and started describing the wine's aromas of flowers and spices. Virgile, for his part, commented on the peppery notes coming through in the finish.

"Here we have the typical features of Rosacker," the winemaker said, chewing his riesling with satisfaction. "This wine comes from heavy clay soil with limestone and dolomite pebbles."

"Lots of minerality," the sommelier pointed out.

Benjamin sniffed the fragrances emanating from his glass, aware that the sommelier was watching him intently.

"I'd say lime, boss. Maybe a hint of tangerine."

"Yes, complex citrus aromas. It's very elegant, practically ethereal. Did you know the name Rosacker comes from the wild roses that used to grow around the vineyards?"

Finally, the sommelier ventured, "At the risk of being mistaken, aren't you Benjamin Cooker?"

The winemaker simply smiled, and with a nod, Virgile confirmed what the young man was thinking.

"We are very honored that you have chosen the Kammerzell House during your stay in Alsace, Mr. Cooker."

"I trust we will enjoy ourselves here," Benjamin said, taking a sip.

At that moment, a beam of light ran through his riesling, accentuating the golden color. Late autumn promised to be flamboyant in this land of Alsace, where the grape harvest sometimes extended all the way to Christmas. Too bad Strasbourg was only a stopover. His thoughts flashed back to the tour guide, Jeanne, so vibrant one minute and dead the next.

"You seem lost in thought," Virgile said. "Are you thinking about that woman who died in the cathedral?"

"Yes, as a matter of fact, I am. Doesn't it strike you as strange, Virgile, to die in a place like that—a cathedral? And the woman was so well informed. It's a shame she couldn't live longer to share her knowledge with more people."

"Educated or illiterate—it's all the same. As my grandfather used to say, no matter how brilliant you are, you can't outsmart death. It must have been her time, boss. And maybe it was fitting that she died in the cathedral that was so much a part of her life."

"Your grandfather—I'm sorry I didn't have the opportunity to meet him before he passed away."

"You would have liked him. I'm glad he was with us for so long and was spry enough to avoid going into a retirement home. He wouldn't set a foot in a church either. He was stubborn, and he insisted on doing things his own way. I think he just willed himself to live longer than most people."

"'A life well spent brings happy death.'"

"He did live a good life, that's for sure. Maybe his sense of humor had something to do with his longevity. When I visited him once, he put on a woebegone face and said, 'Did you know that my old school chum Pierre left us?' 'No, I didn't,' I said. 'What did he die of?' My grandfather looked at me and said, 'He didn't stick around to tell me.'"

Benjamin smiled. Virgile's company was helping him recover his usual cheerfulness. It wasn't so much the tour guide's sudden death that was dragging him down. It was the prospect of vinifying Fritz Loewenberg's Moselle wines. Goldtröpfchen was certainly a beautiful German village set in sloping and magnificently maintained vineyards, but the wine that came from its stocks was too sweet. Making honey from grapes was not Benjamin's cup of tea. He had been clear with Loewenberg and had only accepted the assignment because the man had set his sights on a Saint-Emilion grand cru. The deal was making headway, and Benjamin was lending support to an operation that would cause a stir in Bordeaux. For the German businessman, having a Bordeaux vineyard was a way to restore his image in his Moselle homeland. Bad yeast during vinification had marred his wine the previous year.

It was a matter of spending a week across the Rhine in Germany. Benjamin had used the assignment as an opportunity to visit the hills of Alsace with his assistant, because Virgile was almost completely unfamiliar with its extraordinary wines.

"Tomorrow we'll drive to Colmar. And from there we'll start exploring," Benjamin said before biting into a slice of bread coated with a thick layer of foie gras. "Maybe we'll even go all the way to Ammerschwihr. This matter of the vines cut down with a chainsaw is perplexing, to say the least."

"What happened again?" Virgile asked. "How many plants were cut?"

"One hundred and twenty. All destroyed in a single night."

"Sacrilege! And the papers say the investigators have no leads."

"Reporters are like pathetic winemakers churning out plonk," grumbled Benjamin. "We're lucky if we get half the story."

"Well, it does seem that the cops are having a hard time with this, boss. What are your thoughts?"

Benjamin Cooker wiped his mouth and took two sips of his riesling.

"Clearly, this is an act of vengeance that dates to some deep-rooted rancor."

Virgile, trying to imitate his employer, took one sip of his wine, then a second, and then a third. "This is Alsace," he finally said. "Revenge is bound to be slow in coming, like the late-harvest wines made in this region—and that would certainly wreak havoc. Right, boss?"

"'Late Harvest Havoc.' Sounds like the title of a mystery. Virgile, I think you've inherited your grandfather's wit."

3

On the smooth surface of the Lauch River, a small flat-bottom boat was gliding past the timber-frame houses and cafés without creating so much as a ripple. The boatman, a teenager with curly blond hair and a tanned face, was cheerfully reeling off a historical commentary whose accuracy was questionable. He smiled often at the tourists aboard the old tub, hoping to curry their favor and especially their generosity. He was telling them about the market gardeners who once used the river to transport fruits and vegetables to the thriving market of Colmar.

With a Cuban cigar between his lips, Benjamin Cooker leaned from his high window above a geranium-filled flower box to listen to the young man steering the boat. The view from this hotel vantage point was as grand as a glorious Venetian palazzo.

"At the time, the waterways were safer and faster than the dirt roads, which were overrun with robbers and subject to tolls," Benjamin heard the boatman say. "That's why farmers used the river."

The winemaker imagined the boy as a gondolier with belted pants and a loose shirt, a lean chest, and a cheeky smile. Then he pictured himself gliding along the river, with Elisabeth nestled at his side. His wife often teased him about his romantic bent.

"Benjamin, there's only one person who knows the truth about our marriage: our daughter. Margaux would tell you in a minute that you're the romantic, and I'm the pragmatist," Elisabeth had told him once.

Benjamin had asked Alexandre Bomo, the owner of the Hostellerie Le Maréchal hotel, for the room with the large four-poster bed, "the one on the top floor with the impeccable bedding and extremely soft comforter"—the one whose window opened onto the calm waters of the Lauch.

Benjamin was a frequent visitor here. At every tasting of Alsatian vintages, he would arrive with corkscrews and luggage, settling in on the top floor of Le Maréchal and using the table at the Échevin restaurant as his work desk. The small fried perch was always crusty, the baked foie gras was wonderfully creamy, and the squab was so tender, Benjamin would almost forget to put his fork to the delicate mushroom tart accompanying the dish.

The gondolier and his half-dozen tourists had disappeared under the arch of a bridge. A burst of children's laughter ricocheted off the river. Benjamin closed his eyes and let the cool evening breeze stroke his cheeks. When he opened them again, the residents of the nearby timber-frame houses were turning on their lights. The wine-maker soon began to take in the aromas of soups and pastries wafting from the windows. He fully immersed himself in the moment, when he could vicariously experience the daily rituals of the people who lived here.

His Montecristo was developing notes of leather and, more strangely, wool. The wine-maker watched the gray plumes of smoke as he thought about Jeanne and pictured her again in the cathedral. There was something profoundly unfair about her sudden death. He could still see her glasses, trampled by the crowd, her big bright eyes, her barely loosened chignon, her necklace holding a ring, which he had mistaken for her deceased husband's wedding ring. But Jeanne had never married. At least that's what Father Sebastian, deacon of the Strasbourg Cathedral, had said when he closed her eyes a final time.

"A saint," he had whispered, making the sign of the cross.

Benjamin couldn't get his mind off the woman's death. When he banished Jeanne's image from his brain, the Grim Reaper, banging the femur against the clock of human time, replaced it.

21

The winemaker threw his unfinished cigar into the river and closed the window. He was shivering. A few seconds later, he felt feverish and drained of all energy. He stretched out on his bed and picked up the house phone to call Virgile's room.

"I'm afraid you're on your own tonight," he told his assistant. "I'm planning to turn in early. Enjoy yourself—but don't overdo it."

Benjamin ordered room service: chicken broth and Wattwiller—mineral water from the Haut-Rhin.

The proprietor of Le Maréchal was on the phone to him in a matter of minutes.

"Mr. Cooker, you're eating in tonight? Are you all right? Is there anything we can do for you?"

"Thank you, but there's nothing that a light meal and a good night's rest won't cure," Benjamin answered. "I'll let you know if I need anything."

But despite his best intentions, Benjamin didn't turn out his bedside lamp until three in the morning. *The Confessions of Saint Augustine* finally put an end to his insomnia, and he didn't hear his assistant tiptoe past his room after spending the better part of the night at the Mango, a Colmar club that was open until dawn.

When he awoke, Benjamin felt energized and ready to start the day. But at the appointed hour in the breakfast room, Virgile was conspicuously absent. The winemaker found a young hotel employee whose sagging posture and drooping eyelids suggested that he had spent the night carousing instead of sleeping. Benjamin asked him to go knock on Virgile's door. Three minutes later, the young man returned and gave himself away.

"Sir, Mr. Lanssien is in the shower. We—I mean he—didn't get in until late last night. He wanted me to tell you that he'll be down in a few minutes."

"Are you sure he said 'a few minutes'?" Benjamin asked.

"Um... Well..."

"What I'd really like to know is where you two went slumming last night."

"The Mango, sir."

"I hear it's an excellent place," Benjamin said, stirring his tea. "The girls who go there are said to be very pretty." Then he added, "Young man, might I have a drop of milk in my tea, please? By the way, what is your name?"

"Théodoric, sir. It's not a common name. Everyone here calls me Théo."

"That's too bad. Théodoric is much more charming."

Benjamin repeated the boy's name, trying to get used to the sound of it.

"Ah, Théodoric, I hope you don't think I'm prying, but tell me about the gorgeous brunette Virgile spent the evening with at your club Mango."

"How did you know?"

"Never mind. I just know," Benjamin said, picking up the morning paper and turning to the business section, where he found an article on the wealthy and well-known owner of a Sauternes estate. He had fallen victim to a hostile takeover bid led by his senior partner. Benjamin was acquainted with both men, but they weren't among his close friends.

Benjamin read the whole article, which was quite long. He was surprised to see that the reporter wasn't as well informed as many of his associates in Bordeaux. Anyone who had spent a lifetime in the winemaking business knew that much could be hidden at the bottom of the glass. One had to drink to the dregs. Hugues de Jeanville, the esteemed owner of the Sauternes estate, had not spoken his last. His partner was a hopeless alcoholic and would never succeed in a takeover bid. Time was on Jeanville's side.

When Virgile finally arrived, looking nonchalant with a navy-blue sweater draped over his large shoulders, Benjamin refrained from scolding him. He simply told his assistant to drink his black coffee and eat his two croissants as quickly as possible, because they were expected for an important tasting in less than an hour at Materne Haegelin's estate in Orschwihr. Benjamin wasn't sure this important figure in Alsatian winemaking would be present, but at least two of his three daughters would be there.

In past tastings, when Materne was present, he would invariably wait for Benjamin to finish scribbling in his notebook, put his pen away, and look up to say good-bye. Then, with a touch of modesty, Materne would say, "You know, Mr. Cooker, when you treat your wine with loving care, the wine takes care of you." Benjamin would respond, "Materne, what you have here isn't a wine cellar. It's a field hospital. God knows you nurture your wines." Over the twenty years they had worked together, the exchange had become a ritual.

Benjamin and the Orschwihr winemaker respected and admired each other. Haegelin's daughters had inherited their father's savoir-faire and ingenuity and had learned the business from the ground up. Benjamin always showed his loyalty to the family by kissing the daughters on both cheeks when he greeted them. For the usually reserved Benjamin Cooker, this was a rare show of familiarity and fondness.

"Shit!" Benjamin threw up his arms at the sight of his back tires. Both had been slashed, an infuriatingly malicious act.

"And shit, shit again!" Virgile chimed in. "Boss, someone around here doesn't like you."

The winemaker studied the other cars in the small square across from Le Maréchal. None of them had been vandalized. Benjamin was unable to contain his anger.

"Don't take me for an idiot, Virgile! I know perfectly well where you were last night. I'm used to your escapades, and I also know that you borrowed my convertible to get to that club, where you apparently drew some negative attention."

Virgile, looking stunned, didn't say anything.

"Along with Théo, your partner in crime, you set your sights on some girls and, as you often do, stirred up some jealousies. This is the reason for all our problems. Look no further."

"But I swear," the dazed assistant tried to explain.

"Please, Virgile. Spare me your apologies and lame excuses. There's a limit to my patience!"

"Geez, boss, you've got to believe me. I didn't take the Mercedes to the Mango. The club's right around the corner. Check it out yourself. The car's parked right where you left it yesterday."

"That doesn't prove anything. You could have parked it in the same spot where I left it," Benjamin responded angrily.

"Boss, why would I lie to you? I'd hope you'd know by now that I'm not in the habit of doing that."

"Two tires, Virgile! We're expected at the Materne Haegelin estate. I don't have time for this."

"Let's go find Mr. Bomo and see if there's a Mercedes dealer around here. That would help," Virgile suggested.

Benjamin Cooker continued grumbling about his assistant's "thoughtless behavior" until he thrust his fists into the pockets of his Loden and felt his keychain. He held up the keys.

"I'm sorry, Virgile. I jumped to the wrong conclusion."

Virgile was finally vindicated, and his brazen smile made Benjamin feel even more sheepish. He tried to apologize again, but Virgile was already negotiating with the hotel owner for a car they could drive to the Haegelin estate.

When the hotelier advised Benjamin to file a complaint at the Colmar police station, he just shrugged.

"The cost of replacing those two tires won't be high enough to turn in a claim on my insurance.

And I'm sure the police won't be terribly interested in tracking down the hooligans who did this."

"We live in a far too-permissive society," the hotelier said, sighing. "Don't give it another thought, Mr. Cooker. I'll take care of the tires, and then I'll keep your 280 SL convertible in my own garage. It's close by. Meanwhile, here are the keys to my Toyota. It can handle the steep vineyards of Alsace. Have a good tasting."

On the Rue des Bateliers, the chestnut trees had lost their last brown leaves. The mild breeze coming through the window of the borrowed four-wheel-drive vehicle was like a balm on Benjamin's face, which was still flushed. Virgile was curled up in the passenger seat. He was yawning, and his eyelids looked droopy from lack of sleep, but he was whistling "Habanera" from *Carmen* in an obvious attempt to stay awake.

"Please, Virgile, it's too early, and you're ruining a beautiful aria. Just go ahead and take a nap."

❦

"What bad luck you've had, Mr. Cooker. I hope you're not thinking your whole trip is jinxed," the oldest Haegelin daughter said when she heard about the winemaker's car problems. "We'll have to begin your tasting with the Bollenberg."

"And why is that?" Virgile asked as he studied the golden color of the riesling the Haegelin daughter had just poured for him.

"The Grand Ballon, which is also called the Ballon de Guebwiller, is the apex of the Vosges Mountains. The best wines in Alsace are made on its rounded slopes. Isn't that right, Mr. Cooker? But some people believe the Bollenberg attracts witches."

The young winemaker lowered her voice and continued. "Each summer, on the night between August fourteenth and August fifteenth, pilgrims from all over the region congregate near the chapel at Bollenberg. They light a bonfire and burn an effigy of a witch to banish the evil spirits. Some people say it's an effigy of the devil. I've never seen it myself. Anyway, this year—"

"This year what?" Virgile asked before the storyteller could finish.

"This year it was pouring so hard, it was impossible to set a fire. The rain was coming down in buckets. You couldn't even strike a match."

"And so?"

"People around here aren't as superstitious these days as they used to be, but the witches bonfire still has meaning. It seems that in the years when

29

there's no bonfire, something bad always happens. We might have a bad harvest, or even worse."

"Meaning?" Benjamin asked.

"A big disaster—an epidemic, for example. In 1862, the year before the onset of the great phylloxera blight, they weren't able to burn the effigy because it was raining too hard."

While Virgile hung onto the pretty young woman's every word, Benjamin busied himself with scribbling down the aromas he was picking up in the Haegelin riesling. When he done, he began telling his assistant about the Bollenberg.

"Did you know, Virgile, that the most beautiful flora and fauna in Alsace grow on the slopes of the Bollenberg? More than one hundred and fifty plants have been identified. It's actually a protected area. There are wild tulips, clematis, anemones, orchids, thistles, and more. It's also known for its birds and other wildlife: the buntin, the linnet, and the lark, as well as many insects and reptiles."

Benjamin repressed a sigh when he saw that Virgile was only half-listening to him. He watched as his assistant took a sip of his riesling.

"I have to say the acidity is quite to my liking," Virgile said, smiling at Régine Haegelin and taking another sip. She was holding the long-necked green bottle, ready to pour more if they asked.

Benjamin agreed with Virgile as he chewed his wine. Finally, he delivered the verdict.

"This is a gift from heaven!" he said, emptying the rest of his glass into the spittoon. "Trust me. No witch has touched what I just tasted."

Régine Haegelin handed him a glass of Lippelsberg.

"I hope you're right," she said. "I don't consider myself a superstitious person, but sometimes I feel like knocking on wood, just the same."

"Yes, boss, you can't deny that there's evil in the world. And it can have a human face. Look at Ammerschwihr, at the Ginsmeyers' vineyard: someone destroyed a decade of work in a single night. You can't tell me that this wasn't an evil act."

"Your assistant is right, Mr. Cooker. Whether it's devil's play or God's will, once the damage is done, it's done. Okay, in the case of the Ginsmeyers, you don't feel exactly sorry for them. They're stinking rich. They have beautiful vineyards and a fantastic terroir, and the two sons married well with those Keller twins, who have the most profitable *winstubs* in Riquewihr. The daughter married someone with money too. It's not surprising that they would provoke envy."

"'The spirit of envy can destroy. It can never build.'"

"Who said that, boss?"

"Margaret Thatcher, son. So true in Alsace, as it is in the rest of the world. But let's taste this wine, Virgile. Something tells me it could be the envy of many a winemaker."

Benjamin picked up the glass and gave it a close inspection. The riesling's yellow transparency slowly gave way to infinite emerald reflections. Musky aromas wafted to his nose.

Virgile also picked up his glass, looking like a jeweler appraising a precious stone. Then he plunged his nose into the glass, a part of the process he frequently rushed right past. He was always in a hurry to taste the wine.

"Damn!"

"Virgile! Your language!"

"But, boss, all these aromas take my breath away."

Benjamin said no more and silently watched his assistant taste the Lippelsberg, rolling its freshness and perfectly balanced acidity over his reliable palate.

"Ah, it puts on such a good show," Virgile said when he finished. "Notes of citrus, tropical fruits, lime, grapefruit... Hats off. Truly."

At that exact moment, Materne Haegelin entered the tasting room. It was as if he had been listening at the door. Benjamin gave Virgile a knowing wink, and Virgile emptied his glass in one swallow. But instead of looking pleased with the praise heaped on his wine, the family patriarch was wearing a somber expression.

Régine Haegelin went to her father, who reached for her hand and nervously pressed it to his chest. His own hand was shaking. Benjamin thought of Jeanne, struck down by a heart attack the previous day.

Then the Alsace winemaker straightened his shoulders and walked over to Benjamin, giving him a firm handshake and a pat on the back that spoke volumes about the admiration the two men had for each other.

"Benjamin, I'm delighted to see you. Forgive me for being so downcast. I just found out that someone cut down sixty more vine stocks with a chainsaw. It happened last night in Ribeauvillé. Who would do such a thing, and why?"

"Whose vineyard?" Régine asked.

"The Deutzlers'. No one saw or heard anything."

"Materne, do you think there could be a connection with what happened in Ammerschwihr?" Benjamin asked.

"It's hard to say. The families aren't related. But if that's the case, the idiot sure can get around. Then again, it could be a copycat."

"Let's pray that tomorrow it isn't our turn," said Louise Haegelin, the youngest daughter.

"God help us. I hope not," Materne said. "Régine, would you pour me a glass of our local cognac? It's the medicine I need at the moment."

"Cognac in Alsace?" Virgile said. "I didn't know."

"Yes, it's a witch's brew, you young innocent." Benjamin made a diabolical face and then winked at his assistant. "It's actually pinot noir brandy, finely distilled the way you would distill plums or potatoes. It's nothing like the *eau-de-vie* from Jarnac."

"Call it poor man's cognac," Materne said, drinking the whole glass in a few gulps. "It hits the spot." His pale face began to take on some color, and he smiled at the winemaker. "So, Sir Cooker, where were you? I don't see you drinking anything."

"As a matter of fact, we were finishing the rieslings."

"It's time to get to the Gewürz. Let's start with the best one: the Pfingstberg. What do you say?"

"A work of art. This is an important moment, Virgile," Benjamin announced in anticipation. "This wine is really a cut above, young man!"

Seeing the dark look on Louise's face and Virgile's disapproving expression, the winemaker said, "Um, I'm not sure that's the best term to use under the circumstances."

Materne Haegelin concurred. "You can say that again."

4

Razor-like sheets of rain from the west were attacking the hillsides and mountains. The blue-tinged top of the Grand Ballon was quickly disappearing in the distance. From pointed steeples shrouded in mist, church bells pealed the twelve strokes of noon. The tolling was dull and dreary, reminiscent of a death knell.

The news had spread like a vapor trail. In the cafés and wine cellars, the only topic of conversation was the latest attack, which cast suspicion on everyone.

With one hand on the gearshift and one eye on the rearview mirror, Benjamin Cooker was trying his best to get the hang of the four-wheel-drive vehicle lent by the generous hotelier in Colmar. The winemaker was clumsily shifting gears, overtaxing the brakes, and clutching the steering wheel as if the big vehicle were uncontrollable. Benjamin had left the secondary roads and taken a shortcut on a deeply rutted trail with questionable signage. What did he want to see? Withered grapes hanging from crooked vine stocks awaiting the late harvest? Or was he hoping to catch a glimpse of a mischievous and suspicious-looking character?

Benjamin could sense that Virgile was watching him and enjoying the sight of his boss skidding and trying to avoid the deep puddles and big stones. A couple of times Benjamin had to rock the vehicle out of the mud. Benjamin was already planning his revenge. He'd give his gleeful assistant the job of cleaning the car. Unfortunately, he didn't have time to savor the image of Virgile getting all wet and dirty at the do-it-yourself car wash. He had to swerve to avoid hitting a raging boar followed by her three piglets.

"Damn, that was close," Virgile shouted.

By swerving right, Benjamin had spared the massive beast and her little ones, as well as the vehicle. Unfortunately, one vine stock had suffered from the desperate maneuver. The trunk of the pinot noir stock had been sliced through. The shoots and branches of the eight-year-old plant would soon wither and die. If it hadn't been daytime, someone might have concluded that the damage was the work of the vineyard vandal.

"What an awful day," Benjamin cursed as he pulled a monogrammed handkerchief from a pocket and wiped his sweaty forehead.

The Toyota was stopped, its engine still running.

"You want me to drive, boss? You look like you could use a break."

"I'm fine, Virgile. Just give me a minute to catch my breath." He put his handkerchief back in his pocket, and as he did that, he looked out the driver's-side window. What he saw didn't help him breathe any easier. The vehicle was perched precariously above a steep drop. Below him, rows of vines plunged toward Ribeauvillé. Another bad swerve to avoid an animal or a rock, and it would have been all over. The winemaker began shaking and let go of the steering wheel.

"Are you sure you want to keep driving?" Virgile asked.

"This is too much for a man my age."

"Are you kidding? You did a great job maneuvering in all that confusion! We could have slid off the road and ended our lives here in Alsace. Okay, you sacrificed one vine, but we could have done so much more damage."

"Good Lord, looking down there gave me a scare," the winemaker admitted. He climbed out of the Toyota and inspected the stock. He confirmed that it was the only one that had suffered any damage. The Toyota, meanwhile, seemed to be in good shape—just covered with mud.

"I don't want to sound superstitious, but I can't help thinking that bad luck happens in threes," said Virgile, who had climbed out of the vehicle to join Benjamin.

"Stop it with your unfounded beliefs, son. They make no sense."

"I know, but back in Bergerac, we'd say we've been hit with '*mafrés.*' It means bad luck, a jinx, whatever."

Virgile had told Benjamin all about the superstitions he had been exposed to as a child in southwestern France. And Benjamin had to admit that he went along with some it, even though he himself didn't give such notions much credence. For example, he and Elisabeth would never send a newlywed couple a kitchen knife as a wedding present. According to superstition, a knife could portend the end of a friendship. Benjamin and Elisabeth didn't believe it themselves, but they didn't want the couple to take their gift the wrong way.

"Virgile, just forget your stories of witches and evil spells. What good are all your years of scientific study if you keep hanging on to such nonsense?"

"'Reason is not always right,' my grandmother used to say."

Benjamin had to smile. The boy was hopeless. The rain had let up, and he took off his glasses to wipe the lenses.

Virgile wasn't finished. "She also said, 'When you're sure you're right, you don't need to argue with those who are wrong.'"

"Well, your grandmother was certainly witty," Benjamin said, putting his glasses back on. "Like your grandfather."

"Maybe we should go find the vintner whose stock you amputated," Virgile said, pulling on the windbreaker he had brought with him. "We could go to the town hall in Ribeauvillé. If we look at the land registry we could find the owner."

"I doubt very much that the town hall would be open at noon," Benjamin said, wrapping himself in his Loden before climbing back into the mud-encrusted Toyota. "Everybody's probably out having lunch."

"Well, then, we should get ourselves a bite to eat. I'm starving."

"To tell you the truth, this business has taken away my appetite."

"I think you might be letting it get to you too much, boss. Something to eat would do you some good."

"Son, you're one of the things getting to me right now. Let's just drive into town and see if the land registry office is open."

"That's fine with me, but wasn't it your distant relative, the English playwright and poet, who said, 'After a good meal, one can forgive anybody, even one's own relations'?"

"Oscar Wilde said that?" the winemaker fumed as he put the key in the ignition and released the handbrake.

The car plowed through the mud and finally reached the paved road leading to the village. Benjamin tried to ignore his bad mood and didn't say anything. He was glad Virgile was staying quiet too. The back and forth of the windshield wipers took the place of any conversation.

Approaching the Domaine Bott Frères, Benjamin couldn't resist stopping to say hello to the grand master of the Confrérie Saint-Étienne d'Alsace. Pierre Bott was an old acquaintance. The wines he produced, along with those of his son and grandson, always received high marks in the *Cooker Guide*. Benjamin enjoyed his Osterberg and Gloeckelberg grand crus, and Bott's late harvests had the full and hearty support of Elisabeth, who preferred his wines to many Sauternes. She had Benjamin order her two cases of Tokay pinot gris from the Maison Bott at the beginning of each winter. Her love of earthy cuisine blended perfectly with the smoky notes of this full-bodied wine, which had little to do with its Hungarian counterpart. In fact, the kinship was quite distant. For that matter, in 2007 the European Union officially forbade the use of the name Tokay for the Alsatian pinot gris, so that the Hungarians would stop using the name Médoc for some of their red wines.

Elisabeth was unequalled in her flair for pairing the Maison Bott pinot gris with white meat, Rocamadour cheese, and the duck *foie gras* she bought at the Gascony markets near Samatan and Gimont. For Benjamin, it was a ready excuse to pack the back of the borrowed Toyota. Virgile pursed his lips, but Benjamin pretended not to notice. Yes, he would find a way to get it all into his Mercedes convertible when it was time to go home.

Alas, Pierre Bott was away at a union meeting in Riquewihr. Although he was well past retirement age, this Alsatian man was too stubborn to hand over the job of defending the vineyards promised to his descendants.

His daughter-in-law, Nicole, greeted Benjamin and Virgile. At the Botts' residence, graciousness and hospitality were a way of life. Nicole conducted the transaction with tact, charm, and competence. She invited the winemaker and his assistant to share a simple lunch. Benjamin politely declined, despite Virgile's glare.

"First things first, Virgile," Benjamin whispered when Nicole stepped out of the room for a moment.

When she returned, Benjamin and Virgile tasted the reserve wine, the special cuvées, the grands crus, and also the wines stamped by the Confrérie Saint-Etienne d'Alsace. When his palate grew tired, Benjamin deferred the sparkling wine tasting. But he did ask Nicole to prepare two cases of pinot gris, as well as a case of Gewürztraminer.

"My supply of liqueurs is running seriously low, and Elisabeth makes liberal use of them in her desserts," Benjamin said. "I'd better take a sloe liqueur and also a mirabelle, a quince, and a—"

Virgile finished his sentence. "Williams pear! Mrs. Cooker loves pears."

"You're right, Virgile. But how did you know?"

"She often says that she spoils you by making mostly what you love. Every once in a while, though, she decides to make a dessert that she likes more than you. I'd say you have it pretty good there, boss."

"And I'd say that our marriage and whether I have it good or not aren't your concern, Virgile. Are you spoiling for a fight?"

"Sorry. I'm just hungry."

Benjamin had tucked his tasting notebook into the inner pocket of his Loden. It was a little memo pad with a black fabric cover. The notebook wasn't the one he usually used, but the day wasn't typical either. Everything seemed unusual, even bizarre.

When Benjamin took out his credit card to pay for the purchases, Nicole waved her hand to indicate there would be no money involved. Benjamin balked and even said he wouldn't take the merchandise if he didn't pay for it. Nicole finally gave in and rang up the sale. They walked outside to load the cases into the back of the vehicle.

"Mrs. Bott, I have a question for you," Benjamin said while Virgile hoisted the wine. "Those vines to the northwest, right there, the ones facing us in the middle of Osterberg, who owns them?"

"That depends," Nicole said. "We own the five acres to the right of the telecommunications tower. See that land over there?"

The winemaker shielded his eyes with his hand to get a better look at the area where she was pointing. Virgile did the same. The rain had stopped, and the sky had cleared. The fog banks above the russet vines were drying up like laundry in the sun, and Benjamin could make out the dirt road they had taken to get back to Ribeauvillé after their close call.

"And Deutzlers' vines are on the left. They're on the steepest part of the hill. Did you hear, Mr. Cooker? *He* struck again last night."

"You mean the person who's cutting down the vines?" Benjamin asked.

"Yes, the madman who destroyed the vineyards in Ammerschwihr. Now he's done it again. More than sixty vine stocks. Can you imagine? Who could be mad at the Deutzlers? As if that family hasn't suffered enough."

Benjamin was peeved as he climbed back into the Toyota. There was no doubt about it: the stock he had banged up two hours earlier belonged to the Deutzlers. He needed to make amends without delay.

"Good thing we're going. Otherwise the cops who've been searching for clues since early this morning will find the Toyota's tire tracks up there. And then we'll be up shit creek," Virgile said as if he were reading Benjamin's mind.

"Virgile, stop being so vulgar."

"Our predicament is more important than my language, boss."

"So what do you suggest?" Benjamin demanded.

"Not only do we have to apologize, we also have to compensate the poor man, who must be wondering why someone is so against him."

"Yes, of course. I'm aware of that, Virgile."

The famous winemaker from Bordeaux was feeling uncertain and weary. Too much had happened. And now he had caused harm to a vintner's stock. He drove erratically, his jaw clenched and his lips pursed.

At the roundabout in Ribeauvillé, Virgile once again suggested that they stop somewhere for something to eat.

"Boss, I think your blood sugar's getting low. You need something in your stomach. And I'm starving. Unfortunately, fast-food restaurants are the only places that are open at this time of day."

"Goddammit, Virgile, the only thing you think about is eating."

"Now look who's getting vulgar."

"Forgive me, Virgile. I'm a little upset."

"I agree with that. May I suggest that you turn off your windshield wipers? It stopped raining a while ago. I told you."

"What did you tell me?"

"If it rains before seven, it will cease before eleven. If it rains before eight, it will end very late. Or something like that."

"You're insufferable, Virgile. Your country proverbs are all bull—"

Benjamin bit his tongue, avoiding at the very last moment a word that was not at all like him. At the same time, Virgile urged him to veer to the left. A huge sign with peeling paint near a roadside shrine read:

Fine wines of Alsace
Deutzler & Sons
Owners — Winemakers
68150 Ribeauvillé
(200 meters)

When the Toyota passed through the tall carriage entrance, Benjamin spotted a young man with muscular arms hosing down two barrels. The man looked up and eyed them suspiciously.

A gendarmerie van barred the entrance to the wine cellar and its sign: a stork holding a stemmed glass in its beak. No sooner had the winemaker stepped out of the vehicle than an officious-looking gendarme with a crew cut emerged from the blue van. He marched up to the two visitors.

"We've been waiting for you, Mr. Cooker. To be honest, we were beginning to lose our patience."

5

In the Deutzlers' kitchen, the table was covered with a thick floral oilcloth. A basket of ripe purple figs sat in the middle, next to the open laptop the gendarme had been using to take the notes and statements.

Plaid curtains covered the narrow windows. A single fluorescent light on the ceiling gave the ochre linoleum a milky glimmer, and on the wall, an assortment of burnished copper pots reflected the meager lighting.

The room reeked of sodium hypochlorite. Benjamin could tell as soon as he walked into the kitchen that the Deutzlers used bleach the way sulfur was once used to sterilize wine barrels. Why did the place require such diligent cleaning?

In a misguided attempt to modernize, someone had covered the old—and probably charming—fireplace surround with nondescript porcelain tiles. Hanging from a cord across the top of the firebox were several types of sausages, including black sausages—*schwarzwourschts*—with bacon and *lawerwourschts*, thick liver sausages. On the left, a thick ham awaited the gray days of winter to be picked to the bone.

Benjamin felt his stomach heave as he stared at this display of cooked meats. "Indecent," he said under his breath.

Virgile looked at him and then back at the food. "It makes me dream of sauerkraut, head cheese, and *kugelhopf* with coffee. Remember that Alsatian brasserie in Bordeaux, not far from the old Maritime Exchange, where you took me once? You said you always liked to go there at the end of winter, when the weather was really beginning to get to you."

Before the winemaker could answer, Vincent Deutzler, in a wheelchair, entered the room and maneuvered himself into the spot at the end of the table. With hardly a hello, he cast a wary eye on Benjamin and Virgile. Following him in were two much younger men and a younger woman, all of whom remained standing. The winemaker assumed these were Deutzler's children—two sons and a daughter-in-law from what he knew about the family. Finally, a woman who appeared to be slightly older than the children elbowed her way past the others and slipped behind Deutzler. She put her hand on his shoulder.

The older son was short and puny, and for some odd reason, he reminded Benjamin of a poorly pruned plum tree, neglected in its youth

and then crudely topped off. This son had un-
kempt hair and was wearing a plaid flannel shirt
over a gray T-shirt.

The other son, hardly more than a boy, had
gray eyes, a mop of jet-black hair, and a stooped
posture. Like his older brother, he was thin.
Benjamin could see the shape of his clenched fists
deep in the pockets of his corduroy pants, and he
couldn't miss the sullen look on the young man's
face. Why that look? Was it anger because his
family's vines had been destroyed, or was it something deeper—something chronic?

The young woman seemed friendlier. In fact,
she was smiling. Her face was symmetrical, and
her green eyes and delicate lips were flawless.
Her teeth were pearly, while her skin had the
honey color of someone who spent her summers
drenched in sunlight. Her hair was gathered
under a cap, and she was wearing a short pale-
blue dress. Benjamin couldn't help but notice the
knobby knees below the hemline. How could such
unsightly knees belong to such a perfect creature?
He didn't dare to look at his assistant. He just
hoped Virgile wasn't giving her a too-obvious
once-over. From time to time, she would glance
at the older son in the plaid shirt, but he ignored
her. His wedding band gleamed like the *kugelhopf*
baking pans piled on the buffet, alongside issues

of *La Vigne* magazine and *La Terre*, a weekly Communist-leaning newspaper.

Displayed on the sideboard was a framed color photograph of the family matriarch. She had an oblong face, almond-shaped eyes, and high cheekbones. Her hair was impeccably coiffed. The woman was wearing delicate earrings, glasses with tortoise-shell frames, and a pearl necklace. She looked a bit like Jeanne, but not as kind. Had Mrs. Deutzler also suffered a heart attack?

Benjamin eyed the young woman again. Like the older son, she was wearing a wedding band, but it looked too big for her finger. She kept twisting it. Was it a nervous tic, or did she really want to take it off? She was staring at Virgile, but oddly enough, he wasn't ogling her, as Benjamin had feared. For once, his hunger had trumped his lust, because his eyes were fixed on the fruit in the middle of the table.

And who was the woman with her hand on Deutzler's shoulder? As Benjamin noted her attractive—even beautiful—face and slim figure, she leaned over Deutzler's shoulder and whispered in his ear. The old man nodded.

"We shouldn't let this keep us from drinking a glass of riesling. Right, Captain Roch?" Deutzler said, turning toward his older son. "Iselin, go get us a couple of bottles."

"Of course, father," Iselin said. "Véronique, will you pass the glasses, please?"

Without even looking at her, Iselin disappeared behind a faded striped curtain and quickly returned with two longneck bottles.

All the while, the crew-cut captain and an assistant had also been in the room, waiting for the official business to begin again.

"Mr. Cooker, your arrival is quite timely," Captain Roch said, stepping forward. "We've finished taking Mr. Deutzler's statement. And now we need to ask you a few questions. If you hadn't come here, I would have been obliged to call you to our station."

"On what grounds?" Benjamin asked, taken aback.

"Let's just say a number of coincidences coincide with your arrival in Alsace."

Vincent Deutzler seemed embarrassed by the gendarme's tone. He stopped Roch before he could say any more.

"Captain Roch, I have nothing but admiration for Mr. Cooker, who has always given our wines favorable ratings in the *Cooker Guide*. The only vintage he didn't praise was the 2003, and we deserved that. The vinification was off. I'm sorry, Mr. Cooker, that your tasting isn't taking place under better circumstances."

"Yes, it is unfortunate," Benjamin responded. He turned to Roch. "Sir, can you please tell me exactly what I am suspected of?"

"As if you weren't aware of what's happening around here," Roch answered, staring at the computer instead of looking Benjamin in the eye.

"I don't know if we're talking about the same thing, but I've just come to apologize to Mr. Deutzler for the regrettable damage I inflicted on his vineyard."

The vintner took his glass, which Iselin had filled, and looked around the room. No one said anything. In the corner, a tall grandfather clock seemed to be flirting with destiny.

"To your health, gentlemen," Deutzler finally said. Then he turned to Benjamin. "Hand harvested, of course, slow pressing, vinification at eighteen degrees Celsius with self-regulated temperature, fermentation for three weeks, aging in stainless-steel barrels after cooling, and mutage with sulfur dioxide. No malolactic fermentation. That goes without saying."

The winemaker nodded and poked his nose into the glass of riesling, picking up the notes of grapefruit. Virgile did the same, while Roch and his assistant awkwardly imitated the connoisseurs' ritual.

"What do you think, Captain Roch?" Benjamin asked, looking intently at the man, who seemed to be afraid to say anything in such well-informed company. The winemaker finally broke the silence. "You don't seem to have a very clear opinion about this riesling, which is one of the best I've tasted since we arrived in Alsace."

"To each his own field of expertise, Mr. Cooker."

"Certainly, but a bit of knowledge helps one get closer to the truth. And it is the truth that you're after, isn't it?"

"Naturally," Roch responded.

"In that case, please take this down, as it amounts to my statement. I came to see Mr. Deutzler, certainly to taste his wines, but also to apologize for the damage I caused to one of his vine stocks this morning."

"Explain yourself," Roch demanded. His assistant stopped typing on the laptop and stared at the winemaker.

Benjamin related his story, omitting nothing: the borrowed Toyota, the drive up the badly rutted road, the boar and her offspring, the swerve to avoid hitting them, the effort to find the owner of the land, and the decision to come to this place to compensate the victim or, at the very least, to offer apologies.

"I realize, sir, that you are sorely lacking clues," Benjamin said. "You have no eyewitnesses and, because of the rain, no footprints. As in Ammerschwihr, some criminal took a chainsaw to the vines, yet no one heard anything. You must admit that none of this makes any sense."

Vincent Deutzler stroked his chin, saying nothing.

"But—"

"But this morning, you thought you detected the semblance of a lead when someone reported that he had spotted a Toyota four-wheel-drive vehicle mired in the Deutzler vines. This was quite a development, as far as you were concerned, even though the vehicle plainly bore the logo of a well-known and respected hotel in Colmar, Le Maréchal."

"But—" Glass in hand, Roch was gesticulating wildly in a bumbling attempt to get everyone's attention. Drops of his riesling were hitting the floor.

Benjamin ignored him and continued. "Let's be serious for a moment. Aside from the fact that your suspects would have been practically giving themselves away, using that vehicle, why would they be wandering in the vines in broad daylight, five hours after the incident? Wouldn't the perpetrators have gotten out of there as quickly as they stole in? And please tell me, if you are able, what motive I would have for doing such a terrible thing to this man's vineyard?"

"Your presence at the scene—"

"What happened to the Deutzler vineyard is a terrible crime committed by a crazy person. I realize this man at the head of the table doesn't know me as well as others do, but I believe he can vouch for my character. He will tell you that I am neither crazy nor ill-intentioned." Benjamin was beginning to lose his temper. He put his glass down on the table and took a deep breath to collect himself.

"Still, your being at the scene is troubling," Roch said. "You must admit that, Mr. Cooker."

"Just as troubling as the two tires on my convertible that someone slashed last night."

"As far as I know, the Colmar police haven't gotten any complaint from you."

"That's right. I assumed it was a kid or maybe a drunk—someone hostile to any snobbish outsider driving a vintage Mercedes convertible. Maybe he was mad that the convertible was locked, and he couldn't get anything inside. A common scenario in other parts of France. Isn't that so, Captain?"

"Nevertheless, I advise you to file a complaint with the Colmar police," Roch insisted. "Had you done so already, we could have avoided this little misunderstanding."

"I will do that, because I am convinced now that the vandalism to my car was no coincidence. As for your suspicions regarding my presence on the hill this morning, like you, I am a detective.

But my investigations involve wine, and the scenes I examine are the vineyards. I'm in the vines many days of the year. Just ask my assistant, Virgile. On this day, I was in Mr. Deutzler's vines, although I didn't know they were his at the time. I had heard about the crime, and I was curious. You see, I am a seeker of the truth, Captain Roch, and the truth is often found at the bottom of a glass—or, in this case—under a vine."

Benjamin raised his glass and drained it in two gulps. His fatigue and sadness were gone, and now he felt revived and ready to do battle. This gendarme had no business questioning his integrity.

"I may as well tell you right away, Mr. Deutzler, that your Osterberg will be among my favorites in the next *Cooker Guide*, and please don't think this has anything to do with the initial reason for my visit."

"Let's forget about that, Mr. Cooker. This place is infested with wild boars. Thank God you and your assistant weren't harmed. And, by the way, your young man here looks like a decent sort—handsome too. I thought he was your son at first. He'd make a good son-in-law, wouldn't he?" The old man had a twinkle in his eye.

Virgile flashed a smile at both Deutzler and Véronique, and Benjamin thought of his darling Margaux, who was across the Atlantic in

New York. Safely across the Atlantic. Although Elisabeth had a thing for Virgile and thought he'd make a good match for their daughter, Benjamin knew better. Virgile was irresponsible when it came to women, and there was no way he'd allow his assistant and his Margaux to get serious about each other. Yes, he was fond of Virgile—but not as a son-in-law.

Benjamin looked at Virgile. "You're right, Mr. Deutzler. He is more than a decent assistant. I'd say he's quite gifted at what he does."

"At any rate, I'm glad you made it safely down that hill. One false move, and you would have gone hurtling off the side. I lost a tractor and my legs on that very same slope ten years ago. It tipped over and crashed at the bottom, taking me with it."

Deutzler wheeled himself away from the table to show Benjamin his stumps.

"My legs were too mangled to save. A doctor from Strasbourg amputated them. But gangrene set in, and that put me back even more. I spent months on my back in the hospital, covered with bedsores. There were times I didn't think I would make it. I didn't want to make it.

"But my poor wife, Marie—she was even worse off than I was. She was convinced that I was about to die, and she couldn't stand the thought. She kissed me at the hospital one night and told me she'd be waiting for me. I thought she meant waiting at home, but she meant waiting in death. She slashed her wrists that night. That was long ago, though. Now I have Bernadette, my nurse. She takes good care of me."

The woman behind him smoothed his hair.

There was uncomfortable shuffling in the room. Finally, Roch broke the silence and changed the subject. "You didn't get any threats of any sort?" he asked Deutzler.

"Excuse me, Captain Roch. I have to relieve my bladder. It can't wait." He patted Bernadette's hand, and she pulled his wheelchair away from the table.

Benjamin felt sorry for the old man, who needed so much help. He understood the bleach smell now—there were times "it" probably didn't wait. And yet, at this late juncture in his life the man had found more than a nurse in the woman who tended to him. Apparently, he had found affection, as well.

Everyone watched as the two left the room, the nurse limping slightly.

Roch turned to the younger son, breaking Benjamin's train of thought. "André, has your family received any threats?"

"No, we haven't received any anonymous letters or strange phone calls, if that's what you want to know."

"No quarrels with the neighbors?" Roch asked.

Before André could answer, Deutzler returned to the kitchen and reclaimed his patriarchal spot at the head of the table. Bernadette took her place behind him.

"In Ribeauvillé, just about everyone makes wine," Deutzler said. "If one man's wine is better than his neighbor's, then so be it. Captain Roch, I never had many friends, but until today I didn't think I had any enemies. Now I have to revise my opinion. Sixty plants ruined. It's not the end of the world, but it says a lot about the intentions of this crackpot."

"If I ever get my hands on him, I'll beat the crap out of him," Iselin said.

"It would be very foolish to take matters into your own hands," Roch admonished. "We'll find this person, and he'll face the consequences—legally."

Benjamin tried hard to read in the Deutzlers' expressions and body language what they weren't telling the captain. Véronique had stepped away from the group and gone to sit down without taking so much as a sip of her riesling. She looked nervous, and her hands were placed protectively on her belly.

"Now taste this one," commanded the old man, pointing the neck of the second bottle as if it were a sawed-off shotgun. "It's my son's vintage. Real Alsace muscat! I await your verdict, Mr. Cooker."

The weakling was watching Virgile. Did he have something to fear from Virgile, with his leading-man looks? This was odd, as the *Cooker Guide* had the power to make or break a vintage, and Benjamin was used to all eyes being on him. Virgile stood back and let the master advance his pawns.

"Perhaps it should be a little cooler…"

"You know very well that cold compromises the aromas," replied Iselin, whose unflattering figure made him look all the more arrogant.

"You're right, but only if it's too cold—under ten degrees Celsius," Virgile said. "We're far from that."

"The young man is correct," Deutzler said. "Véronique, could you please get us some chilled glasses?"

Virgile waved his hand, signifying that it wasn't necessary. Then he turned to Roch. "What possible link could there be between the Deutzler family and the Ginsmeyers in Ammerschwihr?"

"If we believe Mr. Deutzler and his sons, none at all. Other than…"

"Other than what?" Virgile said as he fixed his gaze on the daughter-in-law, who had turned pale.

"Other than the fact that Mr. Deutzler's younger son, André here, was in seventh grade in Colmar with the Ginsmeyers' only daughter. You must admit, Mr. Cooker, the connection is tenuous."

"I see," Benjamin said. "Mr. Deutzler, have you and the Ginsmeyers always been cordial with each other?"

"I really don't know them, to tell the truth. I've never even tasted their wine."

"You're depriving yourself of a great pleasure," Benjamin said.

"I'll take your word for it, but Alsace is full of good winemakers. I don't need to tell you that."

"And you, Véronique, have you tasted the wines from the Ginsmeyer estate?" Virgile asked. His candor would have fooled anyone else, but not Benjamin.

"Um, to tell the truth, no. I mean, yes... I think I drank some at the baptism of one of the nephews. I don't remember very well."

Suddenly, she turned as white as a ghost, and her eyes rolled back. Vincent Deutzler's daughter-in-law went limp in her chair.

Roch rushed over and yelled to his colleague, "Call for help."

"I think she'll be fine, Captain," said Benjamin, who remembered Elisabeth's pregnancy with Margaux as though it were yesterday. "It's too warm in here for a young woman in her condition. Let's open the windows and get some air flowing. And, Bernadette, please bring her a glass of water. Did you know about this, Mr. Deutzler? Certainly it should give you a ray of joy in this bleak time."

"As long as it's not the child of the devil," Deutzler sputtered. He moved his hand and spilled his muscat on the table.

"Papa, what an idiot you can be!" Iselin yelled, rushing to open the windows. That done, he went over to Véronique and took her in his arms. He wet her lips with a few drops of muscat, and the sugary scent of verbena and mint water gradually revived her.

6

He loved it perfectly ripened, when the golden crust was nice and firm, and the rind had gone from soft to creamy. As with wine, Benjamin Cooker assessed Munsters with his nose. He'd plunge his knife in to reveal the center of this cheese from the Vosges plateau. The more tenacious and rustic the aroma—even a tad repugnant—the more the cheese lover's nose quivered. To heighten his appreciation, he'd prolong the moment before putting a robust slice on his tongue.

The headwaiter at the Échevin knew all of the winemaker's sensory predilections, but made no show of it. He had therefore cut a double portion and eagerly set it on the dish of this rather exceptional customer.

Ordinarily, Benjamin enjoyed his Munster with a gewürztraminer. The cheese never failed to release the wine's myriad notes of ginger and honeysuckle. This time, however, he ordered a pinot gris, *sélection de grains nobles,* from the Frick winery in Pfaffenheim. The day had been sufficiently eventful to earn him this reward at dinnertime, even if it was a bit syrupy.

"And for you, sir?"

"No, thank you very much. I won't be having any cheese," Virgile said politely.

"My boy, there is something lacking in your upbringing that would almost justify a lawsuit against your parents," Benjamin joked with a full mouth. "A meal like this without cheese is like a cassoulet without sausage."

"Why would I need to set out to sample the more than three hundred cheeses that please the palate when I already know that only one—*chèvre*—can satisfy me? Perhaps if I became your son-in-law, as the old winemaker in Ribeauvillé suggests, I would be more open to the cheese platter."

"That's not for me to decide, Virgile. My daughter's love life is her business alone. I believe she is not indifferent toward you. But at the same time…"

There followed a silence that reflected some embarrassment, or perhaps reserve, on the part of this man of few words when it came to feelings, especially feelings about his family. More to the point, he didn't want to imagine Virgile and Margaux together.

"Virgile, you're busy sowing your oats. Maybe someday you'll settle down, but for now, enjoy yourself—within limits, of course. Your career should still be your priority."

"Maybe you're right," Virgile conceded as he used his knife to push the breadcrumbs from his rolls into a little pile on the tablecloth.

"You know, Virgile, if you were visiting Margaux in New York, you'd have a bread plate and not get your crumbs all over the table."

"I'm making a neat pile, boss. I used to do this all the time when we were eating with my granddad. It took him forever to finish his cheese course, going on and on with his war and hunting stories the whole time. Who needs a plate for bread anyway?"

"I think bread is almost a first course in the United States, and here it's part of the meal. That aside, the fact that you don't like stinky cheeses shouldn't keep you from tasting this incredibly heady pinot gris," Benjamin said.

Virgile didn't need to be cajoled. The two men clinked their glasses as they wished each other health and success. Having taken a first sip and smeared the Munster on his bread, Benjamin launched into a lesson.

"Do you know, son, why we raise a glass to each other's health?"

"No, boss, I confess that I don't. It just seems to make sense when you're enjoying the company and a good glass of wine."

"According to historians, the custom dates to the Middle Ages, when poisonings were quite common. Every nobleman had in his service a taster whose job was ensuring that the nobleman's food wasn't laced with cyanide."

"Yes, now I remember. I did know that."

"Well then, why do we toast?" Benjamin asked.

"I'm waiting for you to tell me."

"When they knocked their pewter mugs together, the mugs would spill into each other. If one of the diners had poisoned another diner's mug, he wouldn't drink the wine, and, therefore, he would expose himself. This is also why, to this day, you must always look each other in the eye when you toast."

With a brisk motion, the waiter, armed with a tiny brush, obliterated the little pile of breadcrumbs Virgile had fashioned, returning the tablecloth to its pristine state. Then he presented the dessert menu. Both Benjamin and Virgile opted for *fraisier à la vanille bourbon*. Benjamin savored the strawberry cake with his late-harvest dessert wine and delivered his reflections on the eventful day.

"This Captain Roch is a little twerp, and his sidekick is his gofer. If they're able to catch our vineyard vandal, you can make me pope."

The winemaker was still fuming that the officer had suspected him for even a moment. The very idea was intolerable. He also hadn't reported the tire slashing. The person who did it would never be found anyway.

The vineyard vandal would continue to commit his crimes with impunity. The incompetent Captain Roch didn't have a clue. The world of wine was steeped in resentments and ulterior motives, and the gendarme was just prattling off clichés. "Revenge is a dish best served cold. There's a story behind that," the crew-cut officer had said when he was leaving the Deutzler home.

"Let's assume he's right," Benjamin said. "Revenge is a dish best served cold. So do you think he'll try to find out who, if anyone, had a longstanding motive to hurt the Deutzler family? I doubt it. Let's see how the papers handle this tomorrow. If it makes the headlines, the police might have enough incentive to put some effort into finding the maniac. One thing's for sure. If the police don't do anything, he'll strike again."

"Boss, who says it's a single individual?"

"You've got a good point there, Virgile. We can't exclude the opposite assumption."

Benjamin used his guillotine to snip off the top off his Lusitania, and a woman at the table across from him gave him a nasty look. Even though smoking in restaurants had been prohibited for some time, Benjamin still forgot.

"You can't even enjoy a good cigar anymore," the winemaker muttered. He smiled at the woman, sniffed the maduro wrapper, and put the cigar in the breast pocket of his tweed jacket.

"Let's go into the lounge and have a plum brandy," he said to Virgile.

"You'll have to go without me, boss. That night at the Mango did me in. I'm beat."

"Amateur." Benjamin was already heading toward the door. Outside, two other men afflicted with the same addiction were inhaling their *puros* with satisfied looks on their faces.

The cold fog wasn't going to dissuade Benjamin from walking through the city at an hour when most of Colmar was still under the covers. In the gray dawn, it seemed that only he and the garbage collectors in their neon-colored uniforms were up and about. He grinned at their shouting and banging with no respect for those who had the luxury of sleeping late.

The aroma of coffee escaped from windows here and there on the Quai de la Poissonnerie. Benjamin peeked into one or two and saw a few people starting their day. And yet, not a single café had raised its metal curtain. The winemaker longed for a hot drink, even if it was a bad cup of tea.

Wrapped in his Loden and a cashmere scarf, Benjamin strolled with a strange familiarity in this city, rich with half-timbered buildings. It had always been like this in Colmar, with its curious seventeenth-century Maison des Têtes and its Flemish inscription, its former customs building, the Koifhus, whose roof resembled the one at the Hospices de Beaune, and the Auguste Bartholdi museum with his sculpture *The World* in the court-yard. And then there was the Isenheim altarpiece at the Unterlinden Museum, which the art lover and man of faith had spent much time studying during his first visit to Colmar twenty-five years earlier.

As Benjamin continued walking, the city slowly came to life again, even though some nighttime revelers hadn't called it quits. On the Quai des Tanneurs, Benjamin passed a group of drunken boys wielding beer cans, one of whom belched a greeting.

Benjamin crossed the street, drawn by the scent of warm bread. He pushed on the bakery door, but the expression on the owner's floury face told him that he needed to wait until exactly seven o'clock. It was no use.

The solitary walker felt friendless in this historic and beautiful town, which, ironically, was known for its modesty. Finally, he wandered to the Saint-Martin Collegiate Church. In a café on the square, the owner of a bistro called Père Tranquille was cranking up his coffee machine.

On the counter, the front page of the morning newspaper announced, "The vine reaper strikes again in Ribeauvillé." A large photo showed the extent of the damage and the look of disappointment on Iselin Deutzler's face.

Despite the scarcity, indeed, complete absence of clues, the journalist had managed to gather a fair amount of information, some of it not to Benjamin's liking. He was annoyed to find that he was mentioned in the article, which took up most of the space above the fold.

"I saw Mr. Cooker with a younger man on that very same slope," one area resident was quoted as saying. "If you ask me, it's very strange that he'd be here so soon after the Ammerschwihr vandalism. What was his business in this part of the country, anyway?"

The journalist claimed that he had tried to reach Benjamin. If that were so, the winemaker wondered, why weren't there any messages for him when he returned to the hotel? It didn't matter. He wouldn't have spoken to the reporter anyway.

Benjamin didn't care for the café's selection of teas, so he ordered a double espresso and two butter croissants. When he accidentally spilled two oily croissant crumbs on the newspaper, the café owner added to the unpleasantness.

"If my first customer mucks up the newspaper the way you are, what will the others say? A little respect, please."

In response, the man from Bordeaux reached into his Loden for a two-euro coin and casually placed it on the counter without even looking at the rude proprietor.

"I didn't mean to offend," the owner said. "I was just trying to make small talk. There's nothing worth reading in the paper anyway."

The café owner was a short and squat man with shifty eyes and a double chin. His bushy eyebrows and downturned mouth gave him a generally sour look. His Alsace accent, meanwhile, was sharper than a Laguiole knife.

"Doesn't it seem strange to you that someone would go around at night bleeding his neighbor's vines?" Benjamin asked.

"I can tell you're not a local, or else you'd know that things like this have always happened. They just didn't get written up in big newspaper stories. Pouring oil and poisons on a neighbor's plants—I've seen that done further back than I can remember. And as far as the Ginsmeyers are concerned, if there are any winemakers. I don't feel sorry for, it's them."

"They don't deserve to be punished because they're successful," Benjamin objected, brushing the croissant crumbs off his wool sweater.

"Oh, we know very well where that success comes from…"

"Meaning what?"

"You are talking, sir, to a pure-blooded son of Ammerschwihr. I could tell you a lot of nasty things about the Ginsmeyers and their so-called success."

The winemaker decided to share a joke to lubricate the café owner's tongue. "You know what Sacha Guitry, the actor, said about success?" he asked.

"No, but I think you're going to tell me," the pudgy bar owner replied.

"'For a man, success is earning more than a woman can spend.'"

"And for a woman?"

"'It's marrying that man!'"

The café owner's face finally lit up with a smile that revealed teeth yellowed by years of smoking.

"When it comes to marriage, the Ginsmeyers know a thing or two."

"There's nothing repugnant about marrying a rich woman," Benjamin said.

"True, but I wouldn't say that about black market dealings with the Germans during the war."

"In Alsace, Germany wasn't really the enemy," Benjamin said.

The café owner's face flushed with anger. "I won't stand by and let you accuse us of that," he thundered.

"World War II was three-quarters of a century ago. For someone bent on revenge, don't you think that's a long time to wait? And how many resistance fighters are still around, anyway?"

"Enmities can go back much further, believe me."

"You've told me either too much or not enough," said Benjamin. "Justify your accusations."

"If the cops did their work better, the culprit would already be locked up."

"Which means that you have your suspicions?"

"Exactly!"

"A name, perhaps?"

"In Ammerschwihr, everyone knows who did it. Consider, sir, that for years, the Ginsmeyers bought the silence of a dozen winemakers by paying them double the market price for their harvests."

"Maybe their grapes were the best?"

"You're kidding. Those people will pay plenty to shut the traps of anyone who knows—or to get good reviews for their wines. They even bought off the guy who writes that guide, the famous..."

"Benjamin Cooker?"

"Yes, that's it. They mentioned him in the paper."

"You have absolutely no evidence that Benjamin Cooker could be bought off. I'd take care, if I were you, about besmirching a man's reputation. Someone could wag a vindictive tongue about your own establishment."

"Then prove to me that what I am telling you isn't true."

"I'd say the burden of proof is on your shoulders. For now, though, let's suppose that this revenge—very belated, you will agree—has something to do with an old, very old, matter. Why would your Robin Hood of the vines—or perhaps one of his offspring—lash out at the Deutzlers, as well?" Benjamin paused, locked eyes with the café owner, and continued. "Given their Jewish ancestry, one couldn't possibly suspect them of collaboration. Am I right?"

The café owner tied a blue apron around his ample waist. "You have a point there, but I know who did it. And I can even tell you that when he was young, he dated Marie Striker—until old Deutzler lured her away. He never got over it, the poor guy. To this day, he's a bachelor."

"If you're sure of everything you're saying, why not go and tell the police?"

"Because, sir, you don't betray the hand that fed you when you were hungry."

Benjamin wasn't satisfied with the man's excuse. But before he could press him, the café owner came up with still another excuse.

"In any case, nobody died. Someone was just getting retribution for a life ruined long ago."

The café owner turned his back to Benjamin to tend to his coffee machine. The man's pants were too small to fit around his middle, and so they loosely rode his hips. Benjamin looked away, fearing what he would see if the pants slipped just a fraction of an inch. The café owner emptied the coffee filter and turned around again. His forehead glistened with sweat.

"Another coffee?"

"Gladly," Benjamin replied.

"I'll tell you one thing..."

"Yes?" the winemaker said, unwrapping a sugar cube.

"Revenge is a dish—"

"—best served cold. I'm familiar with the saying." As far as Benjamin was concerned, the conversation was getting stale.

"Oh, I'm not educated like you, but a little while ago, you tossed out some Sacha Guitry. Well, he also said, 'When a man steals your wife, there's no better revenge than letting him keep her.'"

The man let out a laugh that made his face redder still. "I know what you're up to. You're with the police, aren't you? You don't know me very well. I'm not a snitch. I'm an honest businessman, Mr. ... What was your name?"

"Mr. Cooker. Benjamin Cooker." The wine-maker saluted the bistro owner with his coffee cup. "You know. The Benjamin Cooker who likes getting his palm greased."

7

Perhaps it was because tourist-office representatives from all over France were having a conference in Colmar, or maybe it was because Virgile, unlike Benjamin, had called at the last moment to book his room. Unfortunately, the best rooms at Le Maréchal—the ones with views of the Venice-like Lauch River—were a hundred percent occupied.

Benjamin's assistant had been forced to settle for a cramped room that even a wall covered with mirrors couldn't make look bigger. In addition, the furniture and carpet were worn. But the bed was decent, and Virgile, who was exhausted, fell into a deep sleep, a sleep so deep he couldn't hear the phone ringing just inches from his ear. Finally, he heard it. He sat up, naked, because he always went to bed that way.

"Shit. What time is it?" he groaned, rubbing his eyes.

He reached for the phone.

"We're sorry to wake you, sir, but an investigator from the gendarmes is trying to contact Mr. Cooker. He's not in his room. The night watchman says he left the hotel at six o'clock this morning. Do you have any idea where he could be?"

"Um, honestly, I can't help you at all. What time is it?"

"Almost eight o'clock, sir."

"Okay. Can I have room service bring me some breakfast? With coffee and orange juice? And the morning paper."

"Very well, sir. And what shall I tell the gendarmes?"

"Put the officer on the phone."

Virgile was wide awake now. He listened, saying nothing in response to the officer's news.

Finally he said, "I'll find Mr. Cooker" and hung up.

When the hotel employee arrived with his breakfast, Virgile was still in the shower.

"Please leave the tray on the bed," he said.

"Yes, sir," a woman responded. "Can I do anything else for you?"

Virgile peeked around the shower curtain to get a look at her. The chambermaid was wearing a white blouse that hugged her round breasts and a black miniskirt that revealed shapely legs. He was just a bit embarrassed when the young woman looked up and saw him staring at her.

She left, and Virgile got out of the shower. After drying himself off, he put on a polo shirt, a pair of faded jeans, and his Converses. He drank his coffee and skimmed the front page of the paper. That done, he draped a Shetland wool sweater over his shoulders and was ready to go.

Virgile knew all about his employer's penchant for morning walks. An insomniac, Benjamin was in the habit of wandering about at sunrise and even earlier. He frequently could be found by a river or stream or in a church or cemetery. Those weren't Virgile's haunts. But to each his own, he thought.

After searching the Quai de la Poissonnerie, Virgile followed the Rue des Écoles and then the Rue Saint Jean. He veered onto the Rue des Marchands and was almost struck by a speeding ambulance, its lights flashing. "You'd think they'd turn on the siren," Virgile said to himself just before spotting his boss. Benjamin was leaving the café.

"They're looking everywhere for you, boss!"

"Who's looking for me, son?"

"The gendarmes."

"You mean Roch?"

"Yes, he's been trying to get hold of you. The madman was at it again last night. Thirty pinot noir vine stalks in Eguisheim, at the Klipsherrers' place. And twenty vines at the Flanck estate in Rouffach. It seems the Alsace Wine Trade Council is pressuring the prefect, and they've asked for a meeting with the Ministry of the Interior. They want night patrols deployed from Marlenheim to Thann."

Benjamin listened without saying a word.

"Two television stations in Paris have sent in crews. This business is getting a lot of attention, boss, and Roch has changed his tune. Now he's convinced that you can help him."

"Convinced, is he?" Benjamin said, lighting a little Corona. "And just yesterday I was a suspect. Makes you wonder about his judgment, doesn't it. Well, if he doesn't want to get transferred to Lozère or Guyana, he'd better start hustling."

"What do we do, boss?"

"Nothing."

"What do you mean, nothing?"

"As I said: nothing. Nothing for him, anyway. I do have work on my schedule. This morning I'm planning to rewrite my tasting notes from yesterday, and this afternoon, I'm headed to Germany for the Fritz Loewenberg assignment."

"Roch isn't going to be very happy if you take off for Germany without getting in touch with him. Don't you think—"

"Virgile, since when has the gendarmerie paid your salary?"

"I know, boss, that what Roch did was a slap in the face. To think that you, the creator of the *Cooker Guide*, would do anything to harm a vineyard… To you, pulling up good vines is nothing less than sacrilege."

"I can't tolerate this atmosphere anymore. The distrust is evident everywhere we go. Everyone is suspicious of his neighbor, his winemaker, his pastor, and God knows who else! Let's get out of here, Virgile. We'll come back when things have calmed down. This isn't a good time to be in Alsace."

"On the contrary, boss. I think we've come at just the right time, and I still have a lot to learn about the customs of this land that you described as being so peaceful. Peaceful, my foot! You go on ahead to Goldröpfchen, but I'm staying here. Honestly, you don't need me to do your Moselle vinification."

"Yes, indeed I do, Virgile."

"Give me forty-eight hours. If I have no serious leads, I'll drop the whole thing and meet you. Okay?"

"Good Lord, how did I wind up hiring such an obstinate boy?" Benjamin said, throwing his half-consumed Corona in the gutter.

"So I can stand in as your conscience when you need to take a break," Virgile said, grinning at his boss.

"Not only strong-headed, but impertinent to boot!"

Virgile was already jogging down the pic-
ture-postcard street. The weather was unpre-
dictable at this time of year, but tourists were
still plentiful. They were busy admiring the
merchandise in the shop windows and ducking
into the stores to make their purchases. Above the
shoppers, puffs of smoke hovered over the steeply
pitched rooftops. A couple of storks flew down
and took refuge on one of them. As Virgile rushed
past all of this, two high school girls gave him the
eye and smiled. For once, he didn't notice.

Virgile was convinced that this city was within his grasp. He also knew that despite his boss's
grumpy façade, he had the best of intentions.
Benjamin would undoubtedly give him carte
blanche, provided he delivered results. He would
account for his time. He would have to rent a car,
an economy model, watch what he did and said,
and not do any harm to the Cooker image.

But then he realized that he had one more
thing to do. The winemaker's assistant circled
around the shops and homes and ended up where
he had started. He spotted his boss at the intersec-
tion of the Rue de la Grenouille and the Rue du
Chasseur. Benjamin was just ahead of him and
heading toward Avenue d'Alsace. Virgile whis-
tled twice, and the winemaker turned around,
a surprised look on his face. The young man
gestured toward the Rue du Chasseur. Benjamin

frowned but waited. When Virgile caught up, he took the winemaker by the elbow and led him to the police station.

"Let's make a report about the slashed tires," he said.

"Since when do I take orders from you?" Benjamin said.

"If I can't be your son-in-law, let me at least be your most faithful ally."

Benjamin stared at Virgile, and he thought his boss was about to say something. Instead, the winemaker just shrugged.

"We're here to file a complaint," Benjamin told the duty officer.

"Second door on the left, at the end of the hall. But you'll have to wait. We've got more complaints than usual this morning, and two people are ahead of you…"

Two women of a certain age, one in a gray suit, heels, and a pearl necklace, the other in a stained raincoat, frayed stockings, and a Hermès scarf were sitting on opposite sides of the reception area, glaring at each other. Two boys in handcuffs were on another bench. Virgile had heard them talking, and he thought they were speaking one of the Baltic languages. He didn't know which. He wondered if they were undocumented immigrants destined to be returned to their homeland. As the older one awaited his fate, he stared at the woman in the gray suit while running his hand up and down his sweatpants. The other one was dozing on his shoulder.

"We'll come back another time," Benjamin told the duty officer.

"What was stolen?"

"Nothing. My car was vandalized."

"Windshield? Scratches?" the duty officer asked mechanically.

"The tires were slashed. To be precise, two pneumatic Pirelli tires on my Mercedes convertible. I have reason to believe that the instrument the vandal used was identical to the one wielded by the person or persons who've been chopping down vines all over Alsace, if you follow me."

The duty officer put down his pen and gave Benjamin a hard look.

"I'll go see what I can do for you."

The officer disappeared behind a gray metal door that bore the name Inspector Fauchié.

An officer who had been guarding the boys in handcuffs walked over to the reception desk and slid into the duty officer's seat. He picked up a pen and started going over the papers on a clipboard.

Before long, the first officer emerged from his superior's quarters. Seeing the smile on his face, Virgile surmised that this Inspector Fauchié had given the officer a pat on the back for not sending them away.

"Gentlemen, the inspector will see you. Give him a few moments."

Not even a minute later, Inspector Fauchié opened his door and invited Benjamin and Virgile in. Virgile took one look at him and wondered why the man was still working. He was clearly eligible for retirement. His hair was white, and the backs of his hands were covered with liver spots. He was slightly stooped, but his eyes were keen and ferret-like.

Once they were in his office, the police inspector waved his arm at two chairs and asked the winemaker and his assistant to sit down. Then he summoned a clerk to record the complaint.

"What makes you think that your tires were slashed by something other than an ordinary kitchen or hunting knife?" he asked.

"I'm telling you what the mechanic at the Mercedes dealership told me late yesterday, when I got back to my hotel," Benjamin said. "According to him, only a power tool could make cuts that clean. If you want to verify what he said, have your own people take a look at my tires."

"You're making quite a leap there. Why would the person who's wreaking havoc in the vineyards have reason to vandalize your car?"

"Because there's a connection, Inspector."

"And tell me, Mr. Cooker, what's the connection?"

"Wine, of course!"

"Good Lord, you could be onto something! I forgot that I have an authority on the subject sitting right here in my office. Please forgive me. I drink nothing but water these days—trying to practice a healthy lifestyle, you know."

"That's my attitude, as well, Inspector. As far as I'm concerned, water is absolutely essential. I make it a practice to shower in it every morning." Benjamin turned to Virgile and gave him a discreet wink.

The officer typing the statement grinned at Virgile. The inspector's affectations were comical, indeed.

Fauchié smoothed his hair back and changed his tone.

"Tell me, Mr. Cooker, why are you in Alsace?"

"Writing my guide requires that I travel all over France. I do numerous tastings and familiarize myself with the various terrains and the people who produce our country's wines, both the vintners who go back generations and those who are just starting out. My line of work is more about a philosophy of life than a healthy lifestyle."

"I see. And do you have any enemies? A wine-grower, for example, who may have gotten a bad rating in your guide? I believe you give both high and not-so-high ratings. You have an economic influence that goes well beyond handing out laurels and lashings."

"I never administer a lashing, Inspector. My guide is objective. As for my economic influence, you flatter me."

"I'm only repeating what I read in the papers. A good rating in the *Cooker Guide* guarantees sales, does it not?"

"If that were true, those who get the highest ratings in my guide would be putting me up for canonization. But the wine world is experiencing a crisis without precedent, and I'm no guru. I'm just a man with a lot of requirements whose aim is guiding consumers in their choices."

"All right, Mr. Cooker. Just for the sake of argument, let's eliminate the possibility that the person who slashed your tires was some marginalized individual insulted by the flamboyance of a Mercedes convertible. And, by the way, parking your car on a public square without any surveillance seems rather reckless."

"I grant you that," Benjamin said. "So we were saying…"

"If we reject the first hypothesis, we're looking at a premeditated act that we could classify under the heading 'willful damage.' The question is: who's angry with us. Perhaps you have an idea, Mr. Cooker?"

Virgile was intrigued by the police inspector's line of reasoning, but he couldn't take his eyes off a black-and-white photograph in a black leather frame. Pictured were a bare-chested man—obviously the inspector in his younger days—on a beach, with a smiling woman at his side. The woman, in turn, had her arm around a teenage boy with Down's syndrome.

"Speaking of possible animosities. I've already talked with Captain Roch of the gendarmerie. Tell me: there wouldn't be any rivalry between the gendarmes and the Colmar police, would there?"

Fauchié shrugged halfheartedly. "Theoretically, we always work together."

Benjamin didn't ask the inspector to explain. Instead, he related his encounter with Captain Roch at the Deutzlers. "He's the one who specifically asked me to file a complaint with you regarding the two slashed tires."

"And he was right to do that," Fauchié said. "He'll get a copy of your statement. Would you like to add anything, Mr. Cooker?"

"Yes. I don't mean to interfere in your affairs, but you should interview a man named Séverin Gaesler. He owns a café on the Place de la Cathédrale. An older man, very round and ruddy. At first he doesn't seem very nice, but he's not a bad guy. He said he knows things about the vine cutter."

Virgile was disappointed with his boss. Why hadn't the winemaker told him? Despite his desire to leave Alsace immediately, he was conducting his own investigation at that very moment, and it was even possible that he was one step ahead of everyone else.

"All this can't be the work of a single person. He must have accomplices, or maybe there's a gang of crazies raiding the vineyards just to create havoc," the inspector suggested, fiddling with a paperclip.

Virgile decided it was time to add his own insights.

"So the nutcase—or nutcases—destroyed two vineyards more than twenty miles apart in one night. Of course, it's feasible, but considering all the rain we had yesterday, you'd think the vehicle the perpetrator used would leave tire tracks in the mud. If he parked on a paved road before going into the vines, at least he'd leave footprints."

"To this point, young man, you've been stating the obvious," the inspector said as he motioned to his subordinate to print out the statement so the winemaker could sign it.

"I wouldn't be so quick to dismiss what my assistant is telling you," Benjamin said. "Let's take a closer look at this. Continue, Virgile."

"We have, to date, four attacks in less than a week, and it seems to me the gangrene is spreading. The destruction of thirty, fifty, one hundred vines is not the act of extraterrestrials or supernatural creatures. I know witchcraft is still practiced in your land, but still. The guy in question must be having a blast, considering the way he's screwing you every night. For him, it's almost a game. In my opinion, he has some know-how, because he's good with a chainsaw and he can do his work quietly. I'd guess he's fairly athletic too."

"Okay, Virgile, but that's really not much to work with," said Benjamin.

"Let me finish, boss. I think the guy is acting kind of like an arsonist. The first time, it was to settle a score. Given the uproar the initial crime caused and all the attention he got from the press, the guy decided to take another shot at it and hit harder and better. Like the arsonist who gets more excited the more the forest burns, this guy was getting more exhilarated each time he took a chainsaw to a vineyard."

The inspector leaned in a little closer.

"Now, humor me in my comparison," Virgile continued. "The hills are vast and deserted, and the weather forecaster predicts a strong wind from the south. Soon the idea of setting a fire spreads to other disturbed minds. Little by little, the whole countryside is on fire. Each arsonist is settling scores with little risk of being found out."

"An intriguing theory, Virgile," Benjamin said. "Tell us more."

"Now there's not just one suspect, but many," Virgile continued. "Consider what happens around the Mediterranean some years in the summer. And I don't think a gang is behind this. You'll see. I predict much more chainsaw vandalism in the vineyards. I'm willing to bet on it."

"I, for one, am always reluctant to bet against you, Virgile. Perhaps we shouldn't be looking at the possibility of many culprits, but definitely we should be considering the possibility of two or more."

"Yes," Virgile nearly shouted.

Seemingly unimpressed by Virgile's enthusiasm, Fauchié presented the statement to Benjamin and indicated where it needed to be signed. The winemaker took out his pen and scribbled his signature without even reading it.

"Where can I reach you in the next few hours if I have any more questions?" the inspector asked, getting out of his chair and straightening his shoulders.

Virgile took note of his long neck and skinny legs. Fauchié reminded him of an old featherless wading bird ready to pounce on the first young carp to swim by.

"I'm leaving tomorrow for Germany, but Virgile will be my envoy for another few days."

"In that case, young man, don't hold back what you learn. I'll be eager to take any information you deem pertinent."

"I'm not so sure," Virgile said.

"And why is that? You doubt my sincerity?"

"I wouldn't say that. I'm just not a man who waters down my wine."

"Does that mean I have to convert to wine?"

"Yes, Inspector. I'd advise doing just that," Benjamin said. "And make it red wine. Any man paid to look for criminals has to be familiar with the unique smell of blood. And is wine anything other than the blood of the earth? So you know what you need to do. One to two glasses at each meal."

"And if I don't?"

"Go back and read Louis Pasteur: 'Wine is the most healthful of drinks!'"

When Virgile and his employer took leave of the water drinker, the two undocumented boys were still languishing in the reception area.

The younger one was sleeping, as he had been when Benjamin and Virgile arrived. Virgile wondered how he could do that, because the other one was spitting and shouting at the cops. He couldn't tell exactly what the boy was saying, but he understood swearing enough to know he was strongly advising the cops to go have sex with each other.

Virgile grinned. Maybe then they wouldn't be so full of themselves.

8

The vines descended the mountain in highly regimented rows. They were battalions in golden armor ready to do battle in the valley. But these vines would never cross the Mosel River. Such a maneuver would have been suicidal. Riesling needed exposure to southern sun and a steep incline in slate-rich soil that furrowed in stormy weather. The steeper the slope, the better the wine. It had been this way since the eighteenth century, and no one would have dreamed of experimenting with new vines in the valley near Niederemmel, except to make *Qualitätswein mit Prädikat*, so-called superior quality wines like Kabinett de Moselle.

No one, that is, but Fritz Loewenberg, with his light wines containing less than eight percent alcohol. Loewenberg himself drank only his honey-scented and delightfully sweet Goldtröpfchen, except on certain special occasions. According to some, he was the richest man in Piesport. Benjamin thought this could be true. But the man's production was minor in relation to his ambitions. He had set his sights on Saint Émilion.

"I need that to completely satisfy myself," he had told Benjamin.

Benjamin Cooker had been in Piesport for two days. He was staying in Loewenberg's pretentious mansion with gables and a slate roof. It was filled with ancient armor and tapestries that were tended daily. The furniture, copper pots, and wood floors gleamed. And as far as Benjamin was concerned, the house lacked even an ounce of charm. He couldn't abide the cold Germanic severity.

The night before, he had dined with Fritz Loewenberg. He was a somewhat agreeable man who spoke refined French almost without accent, and he sprinkled his conversation with touches of humor. In truth, the vinification posed no major problems. It was just a little exercise in style for the winemaker from the Gironde, a sort of stroll through the vines on the vertiginous slopes and in the wine warehouses, each of which was polished like a ship's deck. Benjamin's real assignment was boosting the estate's reputation, which the previous cellar master had tarnished. That wouldn't be too hard to accomplish. The job was straightforward and paid well.

More delicate was the role of mediator Loewenberg intended to have him play in the purchase of a premier cru at the gates of the Saint Émilion citadel. For more than twenty years, Benjamin had been the regular wine expert for this château, which was highly coveted by the Bordeaux wine-trade network. Benjamin could intercede on behalf of the German wine producer, guaranteeing that Loewenberg would respect the network's interests in the distribution and sale of the estate's production. Meanwhile, the acquisition would help Loewenberg spread his winemaking investments and serve as a cushion if German wines experienced a decline.

Loewenberg had brought out the most beautiful bottles from his cellar. Despite the businessman's somewhat intimidating bearing, he was a knowledgeable lover of French, Swiss, and Italian wines. His palate was reliable, and so was his judgment. He was assuring Benjamin that the transaction would be a smooth one. Unfortunately, Loewenberg had the bad habit of going on and on.

Benjamin simply nodded every time Loewenberg said, "I'm sure you understand me, Mr. Cooker." Yes, he was enjoying the great vintages, but other than that, the dinner was a boring affair, especially because his host hadn't found it necessary to include any female guests at his table.

It was rumored that Loewenberg's wife had become infatuated with a yacht manufacturer who frequently partied in Monaco. Loewenberg, however, wasn't inclined to make any confessions regarding his marital status. Benjamin idly wondered if more wine might loosen his tongue. He had packed a late-harvest 2010 Fronholz muscat with the intentions of sharing it with this man who aspired to forge a name for himself among the Saint Émilion Jurade, an elite group founded in 1199 by King John Lackland of England. Its members were dedicated to serving as ambassadors for Saint Émilion wines throughout the world.

"Even though your noble ambitions take you from the banks of the Mosel to the banks of the Dordogne, you need to taste this nectar, which is closer to the land you love," Benjamin suggested as he poured the amber wine into his host's glass.

"Gladly!" exclaimed the German winemaker. He brought the glass to his nose and methodically enumerated the perfumes emanating from the Alsace muscat.

"Candied mandarin, orange flower, acacia. Extremely aromatic," he noted.

"I doubt that it ages very well, though," Benjamin said, checking the viscosity of the muscat clinging to the side of his glass.

"All the more reason to drink it right away," said Loewenberg. "Here's to French viticulture."

"It wasn't very long ago that you could have owned these late-harvest wines," the winemaker pointed out with a twinkle in his eye.

"Let's forget the past, Benjamin. Let's drink to the reconciliation of people and the universality of wine."

They smiled and clinked their glasses, but as he sipped his muscat, Benjamin couldn't help musing about the havoc in Alsace. Whole nations could sign sophisticated peace accords, but personal enmities—between families or within families—it seemed, couldn't be resolved with the stroke of a pen.

Benjamin thought about the Deutzlers and his visit the day after the family's vineyard was damaged: Véronique's nervousness and the surly look on Andre's face. What secrets—and sins—was this family hiding?

Virgile called Benjamin every evening. He reported all of his activities, including his conversations with the authorities, the winemakers, their workers, and others. Virgile related what was in the national and local news. On the radio and television, the commentators had dubbed the vandalism "the Alsatian chainsaw massacres."

Unfortunately, the investigation was getting bogged down, despite the long hours Roch and

Fauchié were putting in and the ever-widening blanket of official and unofficial vigilance. Law-enforcement patrols roamed the countryside from dusk till dawn, sometimes venturing onto muddy tracks at the risk of getting stuck and becoming the laughing stock of nearby winegrowers. Winemakers were organizing clandestine meetings and even militias. The prefect was fiercely opposed to these shadow armies that spread out under the cover of darkness, ready to take on any intruders.

When the nights became too chilly and damp, the vigilant winegrowers lit fires on the hills the same way they would on the cold nights of March, when frost threatened the first buds. Some winemakers, experienced hunters, loaded their hounds onto the backs of their pickups and drove into the vineyards and forests in hopes of tracking down the most wanted man in Alsace. It looked like a wild boar hunt, with high tension and much barking and yowling. The sound of gunfire rang out now and then, and someone thought he spied a stocky figure on the Wintzenheim hills. Another person reported that he had seen an intruder crouched in the vineyards near Heiligenstein. In fact, they were deer frightened by the nocturnal circus.

Haughty and authoritarian, Captain Roch led the patrols in the countryside around Colmar, while neighboring police forces patrolled their respective jurisdictions. The Strasbourg prosecutor himself went out one night to observe the operation.

For two nights, all their efforts seemed to be paying off. Nothing happened. But then the assailant struck again, cutting down thirty grapevine plants in the heart of the Osterberg Grand Cru.

Anger rose another notch, and a demonstration involving all the winemakers in Alsace was planned for the following Saturday at the gates of the prefecture. The agricultural trade unions weren't ruling out the possibility of things getting out of hand. Roch, who refused to deal with Virgile, had tried several times to reach Benjamin. The connections between the various vineyards targeted by the chainsaw-wielding attacker or attackers seemed more and more tenuous and, indeed, nonexistent.

Virgile's arsonist theory was becoming increasingly credible to Inspector Fauchié, who invited him to lunch at the Échevin on Saturday.

"Do you think I should go, boss?"

"Of course," Benjamin ordered. He was beside himself with envy. Why hadn't he stayed in Colmar, where he could have enjoyed the food and had more stimulating conversation? At any rate, his assignment in Piesport was coming to an end. He'd be done in a day, two days at the most.

"Anything else?" Benjamin asked, eager to know everything.

"No, boss, just that the archbishop of Strasbourg is officiating at a Mass this Sunday at the Notre Dame Basilica in Thierenbach. He's asking for prayers to stop the evil attacks. I tell you, the devil is getting drunk on riesling and sylvaner."

"Stop joking around like that, Virgile. Go have lunch with Fauchié, and call me as soon as you get back."

Benjamin pulled into the parking lot of Les Violettes Hotel and Spa in Jungholtz, and his arrival did not go unnoticed. Alerted that the winemaker was parking his car, Philippe Bosc came outside to greet his renowned guest. Like the winemaker, he was a lover of vintage cars. He himself had a dozen gleaming touring cars, all of them in perfect condition.

Benjamin was happy to be back in France, with its charming hotels and cordial greetings. Hanza, a friend from Biarritz and a wealthy descendent of industrial pioneer Frederic Japy, had heartily recommended Les Violettes. She was in the habit of spending her fortune in the best hotels on the planet.

This hotel, with its Vosges sandstone facade, was nestled in the small Rimbach Valley and surrounded by the bluish foliage of Le Grand Ballon. From the window of his suite, Benjamin could see the Thierenbach basilica's gray-green onion dome. He had secured a huge room in the style of high-mountain chalets. The rustic woodwork, old beams, antique furniture, and parquet flooring exuded the aroma of beeswax polish. A cozy bed with feather pillows and quilts, thick drapes, and old Persian carpets assured him a peaceful night's sleep.

The road from Germany had been long and tortuous, so Benjamin wasn't inclined to linger in the hotel restaurant, with its elegant but understated décor. But he couldn't resist the Alsatian cuisine, and he finally gave in to the temptation of vegetable *confit* in balsamic truffle vinaigrette, pork jowls braised in pinot noir, and *baba au rhum* in a bath of fresh fruit.

A Gustave Lorentz 2007 Altenberg de Bergheim grand cru riesling, followed by a Blanck "F" pinot noir from the same year accompanied this high-calorie meal. When the clock of Les Violettes struck eleven, Benjamin and the sommelier were still chatting, recalling their latest finds.

A plum brandy, along with a double San Luis Rey Corona smoked on the terrace, brought the winemaker the gratification he had missed during the few days he had spent with the ambitious Fritz Loewenberg.

The following day, Benjamin attended Mass in the impressive Notre-Dame Basilica, a place of pilgrimage for worshippers the world over. He admired the dimensions of the church, the baroque altar carved from Carrara marble, which was bathed in light pouring through four stained-glass windows, and the intricately carved pews. In the end, the archbishop had not made the trip, but had sent a message of encouragement. The priest was on his own.

Women sat in the first pews, while the men chose to sit at the back. The sermon was dogmatic and devoid of the passion that was the hallmark of great orators. Benjamin quickly tired of the repeated references to "the evil beings undermining the persistent efforts of the laborers of the earth." Instead of listening, he looked around the church, first at the ceiling, with its ensemble of holy figures that seemed to be suspended from the arch. He had to search his memory, but he thought he recognized the saints Dagobert II, Casimir, and Francis de Sales. Then he looked at the walls, covered with frescoes by the Alsatian painter Martin Feurstein. Benjamin, a former student at the École des Beaux Arts, admired the *Wedding at Cana* and *Jesus Found in the Temple* for their mastery of light and drapery.

The ancient organ resounded with a medley of discordant notes during communion. Benjamin was not moved. Finally, the priest said the closing prayer, and the basilica emptied. No longer forced to listen to bad music and an uninspired sermon, the winemaker decided to linger. He studied the ex-votos on the walls, which depicted the trials and tribulations of humankind that had been eased by the hand of God.

For Benjamin, the humble testimonies of God's power took on new significance in light of the region's frightening events. Taking his glasses off and putting them on again, he examined each ex-voto in Thierenbach. Their naïveté touched him. He studied the dates of their execution and every embellishment. Then he walked over to a wooden polychrome carving of the Virgin, dated 1350. He picked up one of the prayer cards in a display rack and started reading. It was the Prayer to Our Lady of Hope:

> *Oh, Mary full of grace, immaculate, queen of the universe, queen of the angels and the saints, together with all the friends of this Thierenbach pilgrimage, where we call you Our Lady of Hope, we devote ourselves to you... That in any situation, in any*

burden, confidence in the presence of the resurrected Christ may prevail. We especially entrust to you our families, our friends and all those with whom we work and live. You are our Mother, we are your children today, tomorrow, forever and ever. Amen.

Benjamin slipped the prayer card in his pocket. Once again he studied the Virgin, her grief-stricken face fixed on the dead son in her arms.

The smell of freshly extinguished candles was filling the basilica, reminding Benjamin that it was time to leave. He turned around and exited the church. Outside, the worshippers were busy gathering and spreading the news of the previous night's vandalism near Zinnkoepflé.

Benjamin recognized Vincent Deutzler's nurse. She was wearing a mouse-gray felt hat and a long dark coat. She gave the winemaker a polite smile and shook his hand when he approached her.

"Mr. Cooker, I didn't take you for a religious person."

"You forget that it was Jesus himself who turned water into wine. Wine and Christianity make splendid companions, don't you think?"

"Yes, I do, but now's not the time for wine, at least for me," Bernadette responded. "Maybe you haven't heard. Vincent has left this world."

"Oh no. I'm so sorry." Benjamin was shocked. "What happened?"

"He passed away in his sleep two nights ago. I found him in the morning. I can't believe he's gone."

The nurse took a pristine handkerchief out of her purse and dabbed her eyes. "I thought attending the Mass might help me feel better. Vincent would have wanted me to come."

"I can't believe it," Benjamin said. "This is terrible news. Alphonse de Lamartine said, 'Sometimes one person is missing, and the whole world seems depopulated.' You must be feeling that way."

"It's like we're cursed," Bernadette said.

"Such loss, on top of what happened to the vineyard. Since my visit last week, the list of vine-cutter victims has grown even longer. At least in that regard the family isn't alone in its misfortune," Benjamin said.

"In this case, company is no consolation," Bernadette responded. "But it looks like the police have brought in some guy from Ammerschwihr. Well, not exactly the town, but a nearby village. I heard it on the radio while I was driving over."

"That's surprising, because the person struck the Zinnkoepflé vineyards last night. It's not exactly next door."

"If you want to know what I think, more than one person is behind these crimes."

"I'm inclined to agree with you, Madam... I'm sorry, I only know your first name, Bernadette," said Benjamin.

"Forgive me. I've never properly introduced myself. It's Bernadette Lefonte."

"What will you do now?"

"I'm not sure. I suppose I'll find another client. Unfortunately, in my line of work, clients seem to die off. At any rate, it's past noon, and I'd like to get a bite to eat. Would you like to join me for lunch, Mr. Cooker? I have a reservation at La Ferme aux Moines, right up the road. Their *tartes flambées* are famous."

The winemaker politely declined. He needed a few moments of solitude to digest the news. He shook Bernadette Lefonte's hand and told her he'd contact the family for the funeral arrangements. He watched the nurse walk away. Had Vincent Deutzler cared for her as much as she cared for him? Once again, Benjamin noticed the limp, and a quote popped into his head: "The devil will always be recognized by his limp." Why in the world would that come to mind? Shaking it off, he headed over to the Saint Antoine fountain, near a pond where the fishermen were paying no attention to anything but their hooks and lines.

Benjamin spent a few idle moments watching the goings-on. Then he decided to call Virgile. Had his assistant heard about Vincent Deutzler and the arrest? His cell phone went straight to voice mail. Benjamin called Le Maréchal, and there was no answer on his room phone either.

"Another disastrous night at the Mango," Benjamin grumbled as he walked to his car. He got in, started the car, and took the forest road that led to the clearing where Les Violettes appeared like an invitation to rest the soul.

There was an envelope awaiting him under the door of his room. The winemaker settled into a deep English armchair that reminded him of his father's in their Notting Hill apartment. He grabbed the remote and looked for the local news channel. He finally came across Captain Roch's emaciated face before a sea of microphones.

"Officers have been deployed throughout the region in the effort to stop the vandalism," he was telling the reporters. "But the fact is, we cannot station an officer in each row of vines. The person taken into custody this morning has been released. He had an alibi that was confirmed. At this point, we're back at square one."

Benjamin was actually satisfied with this news. He opened the envelope that had been left under the door. Inside was a flier, folded in two. It advertised power pruning shears that were "highly reliable, easy to use, lightweight, and battery operated." Several models were available, some of which could cut vines, including shoots, branches, and even stumps.

"Quiet, manageable, a battery life of eight hours," the advertisement promised. It included a purchase order.

When Benjamin rushed downstairs to find out who had delivered the envelope, the woman behind the desk told him that a young man had dropped it off during the Mass. He hadn't left his name.

"He took off the way he came, after flashing me an angelic smile," she said. "What I really remember, though, is his shoes. They were all muddy. I had to mop the floor after he left."

9

Virgile was disappointed when Fauchié canceled their lunch at the Échevin at the last minute, citing some "nasty business" he had to tend to. They rescheduled for coffee at ten Sunday morning at the Schwendi, a brasserie on the Grande Rue.

He had wandered in the city all day Saturday, and finally he had gone into the closely monitored vineyards above Riquewihr. In the evening he went to the Mango, where a group of employees from the Maréchal had gathered to forget the tensions of the workweek, with the help of frozen tequilas and Caribbean dance music. Virgile found Théo, who had come with Amina, the chambermaid Virgile had seen in his room. They laughed a lot, danced their hearts out, and drank a little more than they should have. At seven in the morning, Benjamin's right-hand man made it back to his room at the hotel, turned off his cell, unplugged the wall phone, and fell into bed for a quick nap before meeting with Fauchié.

Three hours later, as Virgile made his way to the Schwendi, the sun was warming the air despite a heavy cloud cover. The provincial town was languid. Some couples were buying their Saint Honoré cakes in the pastry shop. The devout were safe and sound in church, and the stray dogs were lazily going through the garbage. Of course, some folks were gearing up for that day's soccer match, but that was predictable, as was the sweet smell of hot croissants wafting onto the brasserie's outside terrace. The business was empty, with the exception of an older woman with a little girl, and Fauchié, who was facing the other direction. He was reading *Le Journal du Dimanche*. On the table in front of him were a cup of coffee, a croissant, and a glass of water.

The inspector looked Virgile up and down, saying nothing about his disheveled mop, haggard face, and late arrival. Virgile was profuse with his apologies, and Fauchié quickly dispelled any unease.

"Coffee?"

"A double, please!"

"Croissant? A *tartine beurrée?*"

"No, thank you," Virgile answered, suppressing a yawn. He still wasn't awake.

When he saw the inspector staring at him, he looked down and noticed that he hadn't tied his shoelaces. Virgile smoothed his wrinkled shirt and ran a hand through his hair.

"That's what they call 'hitting the ground running,' young man!"

"Yep," Virgile said. He changed the subject. "What did your experts say about Mr. Cooker's tires?"

"The Mercedes mechanic was right: the cuts were most likely made by a power tool and certainly not a knife. There were two slashes in each tire, twelve centimeters long, from two different blades. One of the blades could be manipulated up and down, and the other was more or less stationary. In all probability it was a garden tool—actually, a professional tool."

"The theory of the chainsaw is ruled out, then," said Virgile.

"I would say so. Besides, a chainsaw makes too much noise. Considering all the vineyard attacks we've had by now, at least one person would have heard a chainsaw."

Fauchié motioned to the waiter and ordered another strong coffee.

"Are we sure the same tool was used in all the crimes?"

"Roch's experts agree on this point. It's definitely the same weapon."

"You mean the same instrument."

"Weapon, instrument. Call it whatever you like."

"I suppose we can agree, you and I, to think of the individual or individuals as dangerous criminals."

Fauchié didn't say anything. He emptied his second cup of coffee quickly, which spoke volumes about his annoyance with the case. Virgile knew the man had been given next to no authority in the investigation—the gendarmerie had jurisdiction, and Fauchié was with the police.

"So to be absolutely clear, you maintain that all these attacks were committed with the same tool or a similar device," Virgile said.

"Affirmative, except for one detail."

"And what is that?"

"On the night when two vineyards were vandalized, the cuts weren't the same. In one vineyard they were horizontal, and in the other they were diagonal."

"And in the other cases?" Virgile pursued.

"The cuts were diagonal most of the time, and they appeared to start on the same side of the vine. What do you make of that, Virgile?"

"At the risk of contradicting myself, it could be one guy who has help from an accomplice on occasion."

"That's my opinion, too," Fauchié said.

Virgile looked up when he heard chairs scraping the floor. The older woman and the little girl were getting up to leave. Virgile smiled at the child when he saw her mouth, all covered with hot chocolate and whipped cream. The little girl started smiling back, but her grandmother had grabbed a napkin to clean her up. When she was done, the girl stuck her pink tongue out at Fauchié. Her grandmother grabbed her hand and apologized.

"When parents don't provide their children with the proper upbringing, that's what you get: little devils! Arielle, apologize to the gentleman."

The little girl was frowning at Fauchié.

"No, Grand-mere! He's gross."

The embarrassed grandmother turned around and started walking out, dragging the insolent child behind her.

"Wait till we get home, young lady," Virgile heard her say. "You'll be in timeout. Your parents may let you get away with anything. But you're with me now."

Inspector Fauchié didn't appear offended. But when Virgile looked at him a few moments too long, he stiffened and seemed to lose his self-confidence.

"Children can be so inconsiderate," Virgile ventured.

"I'm no expert when it comes to children, Virgile. I never had any of my own."

"So that wasn't you in the picture I saw in your office?"

"It was. I married a woman who had a child, and I raised him as my own son."

A cloud of melancholy seemed to settle over the inspector, and Virgile made an attempt to lighten the mood. "What's his name?" he asked.

"Damien. He has Down's syndrome and lives in a work-based support center in Divonne-les-Bains, in the Jura mountains. We go to see him every other Sunday. You see, last Sunday I wouldn't have been able to meet you here."

The man smoothed his white hair with his speckled hands. Virgile had noticed that the inspector's hair was unusually long at the nape of his neck. Still, it didn't completely hide the large wine-colored birthmark.

Fauchié talked about Damien with both tenderness and sadness. He had never experienced the joys of fatherhood that other men took for granted: Sunday afternoon soccer games, study sessions at the kitchen table, dating tips, the search for the right college... Damien would never marry and make him a grandfather. In fact, because his son also had health problems, the boy would probably die before he did.

"This is how it's been for twenty-eight years, Virgile. I've lived with Down's syndrome since the day I married. But I wouldn't change my life for anything. Happiness lies with the people you love."

The inspector's face brightened. The fine crow's feet made his moss-green eyes more mischievous and his whole appearance less austere. His teeth were perfect for a person his age, and his lips were finely shaped.

Virgile smiled. His grandmother would have had an expression for the inspector: "a handsome man in his day."

"A third coffee would not be reasonable, would it?" Fauchié suggested.

"Reasonable people are a pain in the ass," Virgile replied, flashing his own mischievous eyes.

Thanks to the coffee and the conversation, Virgile was no longer feeling the effects of his night on the town and his lack of sleep. He felt energized and eager to find the "vine assassin," which was what at least one newspaper was calling him.

"I just thought of something, Inspector. Judging by my observations at the Klipsherrer, Flanck, Deutzler, and Ginsmeyer vineyards, it would seem that our weirdo goes after relatively young vines: five years old—ten at the most."

"That's true," Fauchié confirmed. "I hadn't given it much consideration."

"In that case, he's a professional!"

"Well, he is now: he's attacked five vineyards," the inspector said.

"No, that's not what I mean," said Virgile. "He's in the profession: he's a winemaker."

"What makes you say that?"

"First of all, destroying a budding vine is more exciting than killing an old vine. Second, young plants are easier to prune than gnarly ones. And for that, there are extremely sophisticated power pruners these days. They're sharp, lightweight, and quiet. Models for left-handed people are even available."

"If I follow your line of reasoning, you may be trying to convince me that we're dealing with some kind of winemaker's vengeance scheme and not a madman who takes pleasure in reading about his misdeeds in the papers."

"Power pruning shears are a tool a winemaker would use, and I'm tempted to add a young wine-maker, because some of the old guys still balk at them. They're rather expensive, but you can do a season's worth of pruning in a matter of days. In the Bordeaux and Burgundy regions, power pruners replaced the manual ones long ago."

"I take it they're battery operated. How do they work?"

"It's easy: the shears look like classic pruners, except they're more responsive. They're connected to a lithium battery pack that you wear on your belt or on your back. The wire connecting the shears and the battery pack doesn't restrict your movements in any way."

"And what about the battery? It must weigh a ton."

"Not really. It depends on the model. It can weigh anywhere from two and a half to five kilos. Sure, at the end of the day you feel it, but compared with the tendinitis you can get with manual shears, the weight is hardly a problem."

"Do you know how to use one of these things?"

"Yes. It feels a little like a gun, and you have to be careful about not cutting the wire that connects the shears to the battery pack. But once you get the hang of it, you can cut everything: vine shoots, spurs, vine stocks…"

"What kind of safety precautions do you need to take?" Fauchié asked.

"Not many. They just pinched my fingers at first. You'd have to be really clumsy to cut yourself. Steel-mesh gloves are available to protect your hands, but they're a little like boxing gloves. I'd never wear them."

"In short, you could say we've identified the weapon, which gives us some information about the perpetrator."

"You could say that. But we're still very far from apprehending a suspect."

Before he could express any more doubts, Virgile heard a commotion on the Grand Rue. He looked up and saw scores of people marching down the street. They were all dressed in their Sunday best: Burberry coats and Hermès scarves.

A few minutes later, the church bells started pealing. The late Sunday Mass.

"You don't attend, Inspector?" Virgile asked.

"No, I find my inspiration in the Sunday paper. And you?"

"I can't say I'm a regular churchgoer either. I prefer my sleep on Sunday mornings."

Just as quickly, the streetscape emptied again. Only a bedraggled man searching for coins on the ground remained in the square. Every once in a while a bicyclist would whiz by, his shrill bell grazing the silence.

But Colmar was beginning to stir. Soon, the good Catholics would emerge from church and start visiting the bakeries and candy stores, where they would purchase goodies to take home. Later in the afternoon, if their children were well behaved, they'd take them for lakeside outings at Altenweiher or Fischboedle.

Fauchié and Virgile fell silent, as if to enjoy these moments when the Alsatian city was still holding its breath.

"Did you hear about Vincent Deutzler?" Fauchié finally said.

"No. What about him?"

"He died in his sleep two nights ago. Looks like natural causes. But the family has asked for an autopsy."

"Do they have any reason to be suspicious? He was getting on, and the destruction of his vineyard had to hit him hard. It wouldn't be surprising if he suffered a heart attack in his sleep."

"I can't answer that question. The family might know something that we don't. At any rate, if the autopsy confirms natural causes, they'll be able to bury their father in peace."

"I feel sorry for the Deutzlers. They've lost so much."

"And his isn't the only death. Old Séverin Gaesler, who owned the bistro over there, kicked the bucket last night. A stroke or a heart attack. Maybe both."

"Were you able to question him before he died?" Virgile asked.

"I went to the hospital twice. The first time, he was out of it. The second time, he had trouble talking and didn't seem to understand what I was asking him. The doctors said his brain wasn't getting an adequate blood flow. They were hoping he'd eventually regain some of his faculties. Anyway, if he had any secrets, he's taken them to the grave," Fauchié said, sighing. "Say, it's past time for coffee. How about a beer?"

"I'm up for that," Virgile answered.

"Brown or blond? French or German," the inspector asked as if he were conducting an interrogation.

"A Bitburger, please. I'm partial to light beers. And you?"

"Me? Today I'm having a whiskey. Healthy lifestyle be damned."

"Healthy or not, I like your style, Inspector."

The two men smiled each other, and Virgile went back to Gaesler. "If the guy from Ammerschwihr, the one Gaesler told my boss about, was the perpetrator, he'd be too old to be traipsing through the countryside at night, armed with a set of power shears. And even if this person was hearty enough to be cutting down the vines, why would he attack properties owned by families that were never suspected of collaboration? No, I think Gaesler was an inveterate liar. A storyteller, like all café owners."

"I'm inclined to agree with you, especially because I relayed your boss's information to Captain Roch, and the three confirmed bachelors identified in the Ammerschwihr commune all claimed they didn't know Gaesler. None of them had any dispute with the Ginsmeyers. One of them is in a retirement home. The second lives half the time with his sister in Kaysersberg. As for the third, he's had two strokes and can't use one of his arms."

"So, as I said, Gaesler's story doesn't hold up," Virgile concluded.

"Have funeral arrangements for Deutzler and Gaesler been made?"

"Gaesler's is at ten thirty Tuesday. Deutzler's will depend on the autopsy. Are you planning to attend the services?"

"I don't know if I'll be there, but I'm sure my boss will make an appearance at both of them."

"Why is that?"

"He always goes to funerals."

"That's unusual—attending the funeral of someone you hardly know just for the sake of going," Fauchié said. "Some people would say it's morbid."

"Mr. Cooker says the dead speak to him."

Fauchié drank the rest of his whiskey. He glanced at his watch and suddenly looked worried.

"I promised my wife I'd... Can I drop you off somewhere, Virgile?"

Virgile politely declined and said good-bye. He put down his beer and headed for the nearby café Gaesler had owned.

On the doorstep of the Père Tranquille, someone had left a bouquet of white yarrow.

10

A ravenous crowd had descended on La Ferme aux Moines. Benjamin took one look at all the patrons, who just a few hours earlier were in church, begging the Almighty to drive the vine cutter from their land, and wondered if they had been fasting a whole week in their effort to banish the evildoer. More than three hundred people were elbow-to-elbow in the immense refectory, which specialized in buffets.

Massive and rustic-looking wrought-iron chandeliers hung above long wooden tables, where patrons—too eager to dig in to give saying grace a second thought—filled themselves with *tartes flambées*, braised sauerkraut, and perch in wine sauce. On the walls, three-dimensional accents depicted Benedictine monks and craftsmen going about their daily duties, which involved the fruit of the vine and good food.

Benjamin spotted Bernadette Lefonte eating by herself. He didn't care to join her, so he worked his way to the other side of the room, found a seat behind a pillar, and tried to avoid making eye contact.

The winemaker wasn't all that hungry. Without enthusiasm and without even consulting the menu, he ordered a duck and sour cherry terrine and a veal fillet served with girolle mushrooms. Then he pulled out the flier and examined all the power tool's technical details.

He was familiar with power shears, successor to the pneumatic shears, although he himself had always refused to use them. No doubt the flier bore a message. Someone wanted him to know the identity of the weapon used in the vineyard vandalisms. But not that many people were aware that he was here in Thierenbach and staying at Les Violettes. Benjamin couldn't think of a single person who could have left it, except...

To accompany his veal fillet and add a note of humor to his meal, Benjamin ordered a glass of Fumant de la Sorcière—Smoking Witch wine made by Pierre Meyer of Orschwihr.

When Virgile burst into the refectory, most of the overdressed customers had left to go strolling along the Route des Crêtes, toward the Alsace hills. It was unseasonably warm outside, far too nice to remain in the dimly lit Ferme aux Moines.

Having finished his wine and dinner, Benjamin was sipping his tepid coffee. He waved to Virgile, who was hurrying toward him, looking famished and excited.

"Boss, I've been searching for you for two hours! I checked the hotel first thing. They told me you were 'on a pilgrimage.' God knows where. I looked all over and went back to your hotel. Then they told me that you had gone up to your room, only to hurry out a few minutes later."

"Virgile, are you the one who left me this flier?"

"Yeah," said the young man, already seated and expecting to be served. "I found it in a hardware store in Colmar yesterday. And I'm afraid I left a trail of mud in the lobby of your hotel. I got my Converses pretty dirty in the vineyards."

"I presume you haven't had anything to eat?"

"No. I had coffee with Inspector Fauchié this morning. I'm starving!"

"I'm afraid they've stopped serving, Virgile. Maybe you can charm a waitress into scaring up something for you in the kitchen."

Virgile negotiated a *tarte flambée* and a Château Monastique beer, but not from the young Alsatian woman with the turned-up nose who was clearing the tables and snuffing out the big candles. Rather, it was a boy with a silly grin who worked in both the kitchen and the dining room who took his order.

Meanwhile, the winemaker had taken a Quai d'Orsay Imperiales from his leather case. The Havana had been carefully rolled in a Cuban factory and brought back into fashion by its

French importer. He intended to smoke the cigar later, after Virgile had finished reporting all the conclusions of his independent investigation.

Benjamin took pleasure in watching Virgile devour his extra-large portion of *tarte flambée* as though he were celebrating the end of Lent. Happy to be reunited with his sidekick, the wine-maker ordered a glass of chartreuse liqueur to better enjoy Virgile's revelations.

But instead of conclusions, the conversation was soon filled with conjecture. Benjamin was angry with himself for not grilling Gaesler the morning he visited the café. Now he'd have to start from scratch. He was inclined to believe that the Ammerschwihr vandalism, along with the others, had nothing to do with the war. But he hadn't ruled out the possibility. And Roch didn't have a clue. He had abandoned the lead altogether, saying any suspected culprits were far too old.

"In the countryside, Virgile, grudges can go on for generations, and it's always the most disreputable family member who refuels an old quarrel. A grudge over a torn-down boundary marker, a blind horse sold at full price, or a grape picker who abandoned a neighbor's daughter can be passed down from grandfather, to son, and finally to grandson. Some grudges can go back much further. As Paul Gauguin said, 'Life being what it is, one dreams of revenge.'"

"You're telling me? I know all about resentment in rural life."

"Of course you do, but you're too good-hearted, son, to understand the rancor that motivates those the world rejects."

"Still, there's no evidence to show that any of those destroyed vines were owned by the descendants of collaborators. Fauchié is clear on that point. The Kipsherrers in Eguisheim bought their property ten years ago, after making a fortune in the Yellow Valley in Australia. The Flancks had two family members who died at Buchenwald. I don't think you can accuse them of sleeping with the enemy. No, boss, following that lead will get us nowhere. So we're left with the weapon as our lead."

"Agreed," Benjamin said. "But Koch isn't about to call in all the owners of power shears. Only catching someone in the act will save him."

"A little lesson on viticulture, boss. How many acres of vineyards are there in Alsace?"

Benjamin appreciated his assistant's quick thinking and didn't take offense when his youthful manner bordered on insolence.

"I'd say a little over thirty-seven thousand acres," the winemaker replied.

"Precisely! You wouldn't happen to be the creator of France's most authoritative guidebook on wines, would you?"

Benjamin smiled and looked around. La Ferme aux Moines had emptied out.

"Let's go for a walk, Virgile. I'd like to enjoy my cigar, and I want to take another look at the church."

Benjamin blinked in the bright sunlight. As they headed toward the church, its onion dome gleaming, the winemaker and his assistant continued to discuss the case.

"I understand Roch has called for reinforcements," Benjamin said. "It seems this matter is greatly irritating the higher-ups in Paris. The minister of the interior was summoned by the prime minister just this morning."

"So?" asked Virgile.

"So, I don't think that a Mass like this morning's will make any difference. I think our madman will either take a break, or else he'll walk into the lion's den."

"I'm willing to bet he'll strike again. What will you wager, boss?"

"I'd bet a bottle of Albert Seltz's Zotzenberg grand cru sylvaner—late harvest," Benjamin answered before taking two puffs of his Imperiales. They had reached the square in front of the basilica.

"Do you want to ruin me, boss?"

"One must either be sure of his instincts or keep quiet," Benjamin answered.

"I'd agree with you on that score. But some people's instincts are way off. Take Roch. His men busted that young hunter and then had to release him. The poor fellow was just rendezvousing behind the chapel of the Quatorze-Auxiliaires. Not exactly a good place to screw, if you ask me. He accidentally set off the bird cannon. That's why they went after him."

"He set off the bird cannon? That part of the story wasn't in the news. You have some good sources, Virgile."

"Fauchié told me this morning. Yeah, there are so many birds up there trying to loot the grapes, they installed those repeaters near the chapel to scare them away. Considering the price of a bottle of grand cru Steinklotz, you can imagine the damage the birds can do."

The winemaker nodded. "I'm glad the boy was cleared so quickly."

"It seems he had more than one thing going for him. And they wound up causing our gendarme a lot of embarrassment," Virgile said. "The hunter is also a volunteer firefighter, and the night the vines in Ammerschwihr were attacked, he was called to an accident in some godforsaken place to extricate a poor guy from his car. As for the other..."

"Yes?" Benjamin urged his assistant on as he played with his cigar.

"The woman he was with was none other than the wife of the president of the local wine cellar. It was a big scandal. Said president convinced Roch that the guy in question was the one he was looking for. And Roch didn't bother to do his legwork. All he wanted to do was appease the prefecture. But it backfired, and the higher-ups were very unhappy when they learned what Roch was doing. I think you were right when you predicted that he would soon end his career in Lozère or in Guyana."

"What does Fauchié think of Roch?"

"In my opinion, he doesn't hold him in high esteem."

"Perfect. Tomorrow, let's go back to Colmar. I know there are a few samples waiting for me at Le Maréchal. And then we'll decide."

"Why not go back right now?" Virgile asked.

"Because you don't turn down the opportunity to spend a night at Les Violettes. Also, I'd like to show you the owner's collection of roadsters. Real gems, with engines that run like clockwork. And since there aren't any nightclubs for twenty miles around, I'm sure you'll get a good night's sleep."

"That's a plan," Virgile agreed.

"Glad to hear it."

No sooner had Benjamin said this than he started feeling woozy. He lost his footing as he began climbing the stairs to the church, and a second later he was sprawled at his assistant's feet.

"Are you all right, boss? That was a nasty spill."

Virgile helped the winemaker get back on his feet. Benjamin felt his left hip and elbow, brushed off his Loden, and didn't bother to pick up his half-consumed cigar, which had rolled like a Musketeer's rapier to the bottom of the monumental staircase.

"I seem to be in one piece, although I'll probably have a bruise or two tomorrow."

"What happened?"

"Nothing, Virgile, nothing. Just a little dizzy spell..."

"Are you sure? You didn't break anything? This streak of bad luck is lasting a bit too long, if you ask me."

"I'm fine. Let's just go back to the hotel."

"You seem to be limping, boss."

"As I said, Virgile, I'm fine!"

Annoyed, Benjamin declined Virgile's invitation to take his rented car back to the hotel.

"I'll just walk, Virgile. The hotel's close by. You go on ahead of me."

Benjamin waved his assistant good-bye and waited for him to take off before he started walking back to Les Violettes. He didn't want Virgile to see that he was, indeed, limping.

11

Dr. Gildas Cayla
General Medicine
Office Hours: 9:00 a.m. to 12:30 p.m.
House Calls: Afternoons

The mottled-brass plaque had to date back to the opening of the esteemed doctor's office at 15 Rue des Tonneliers in Ribeauvillé. Nearly lost on a façade covered with ampelopsis vines, the sign, it seemed, hadn't been polished in ages.

The physician's reputation was well established, according to those who had recommended him, and his office was never empty. Faithful to the spirit of country doctors, he treated poor patients free of charge. Never, ever, would Dr. Cayla be responsible for the endemic deficit of the National Health Care System.

"Wait for me in the café across the street," Benjamin told Virgile as he extricated himself from the convertible with some difficulty.

"Don't you want me to go with you, just to keep you company if you wind up waiting three hours to be seen?"

"Go on, I said! And stop treating me like a cripple."

Despite his bum leg, Benjamin had already disappeared behind the heavy door with a magnificent wrought-iron knocker.

Why the devil are waiting rooms so inhospitable, Benjamin wondered as he took in Dr. Cayla's office. A dozen uncomfortable-looking chairs lined the walls. Ragged gossip magazines were piled on a low table in a corner, and under a window that lacked curtains, a dried ficus begged for water, if only a few drops. Three other people were waiting.

"Hello," the winemaker said, trying to sound cheerful. Two people looked up from their magazines. The third didn't bother. His eyes were glued to his cell phone. He appeared to be a businessman, as he was wearing a gray three-piece suit. He was thin, and his coloring was sallow. To his left, a girl with short hair, a navy-blue sweater, and tight white pants reminded Benjamin of the actress Jean Seberg, one of his favorites. The third patient gave Benjamin a surprised look.

"Why, hello," she said, venturing a smile.

Although her eyes were the same lichen color, her face was gaunt and white. Her right arm was in a sling, and Vincent Deutzler's daughter-in-law seemed to have lost the youthful charm he had seen the day he had visited the home of the Ribeauvillé winemaker.

"What happened to your arm?" Benjamin asked as he slowly lowered himself into one of the rigid chairs. He was careful to keep the leg that was throbbing fully extended. He felt a bit ridiculous, as he couldn't get his Lobb on the bad foot. He had been forced to wear his wool slipper.

"Nothing serious," the Deutzler daughter-in-law answered tersely. "Just a little problem with my wrist. The doctor thinks it's a flare-up of my carpal tunnel."

"Carpal tunnel at your age?" Benjamin asked.

"Yes, it comes and goes."

"I'm sorry," Benjamin said. "I was also saddened to hear about your father-in-law. How are you holding up?"

"We're all right. Thank you for asking." Véronique lowered her eyes and plunged back into her gossip magazine.

Benjamin eyed the young woman, recalling she was pregnant, and smiled, remembering the joy he felt when he held Margaux in his arms for the first time. Then he winced. The pain in his right foot was getting worse. Strain, sprain, dislocation, fracture—all these terms danced in his head. He dreaded Dr. Cayla's verdict, although he knew nothing of the man in whose hands he was entrusting himself.

He thought about picking up one of the magazines, but he had no interest in celebrities and their cheating scandals. Why didn't doctors ever have anything more intellectually stimulating to read? Like the man in the three-piece suit, would he have to resort to checking his e-mails and browsing the Internet on his cell phone? Benjamin groused to himself and looked around the room for something to catch his attention.

The door to the inner sanctum opened. "Mr. Hamecher? Dr. Cayla will see you now. How are you doing today?"

Fifteen minutes later, Mr. Hamecher walked out of the office, and the inner door opened again. The receptionist beckoned to a woman named Mrs. Koenig.

Like clockwork, Mrs. Koenig emerged fifteen minutes later, and Deutzler's daughter-in-law was ushered in. She rose from her chair and gave Benjamin a nod before walking through the door. This consultation, however, lasted longer than fifteen minutes—much longer. Benjamin took heart in the time Gildas Cayla was spending with the young woman. It appeared that when a patient needed extra attention, he gave it.

When it was the winemaker's turn, Benjamin hobbled in, taking care not to put too much weight on his foot. Dr. Cayla, bald and bespectacled, shook Benjamin's hand, but instead of asking him why he was limping, he stared at his face.

"Maybe my age is playing tricks on me, but you remind me of a man I saw recently on television. He was talking about wine. His name was Déquerre or something like that. He comes out with a book every year on the best wines in each region of France."

"Cooker," Benjamin said, correcting the doctor.

"Yes, that's it. Your resemblance to each other is as close as two drops of water."

"… of wine, you mean."

"Excuse me? I'm a little hard of hearing."

"Like two drops of wine," Benjamin said, not displeased that his reputation had gained him a certain following in the medical profession. The winemaker had recently experienced a similar encounter with a physician in the Beaujolais region.

"Oh my, I can't believe it. Benjamin Cooker right here in my office," Gildas Cayla enthused. "If someone had predicted that one day the greatest wine expert would come to see me as a patient, I never would have believed him."

"Let's not exaggerate," said Benjamin, who, in fact, felt a tad embarrassed every time someone called him the greatest wine expert. "Today I'm merely your patient—a patient who knows full well that stemmed wine glasses sometimes break, the same way our own legs can fail us from time to time."

"So tell me. What happened?"

The winemaker told the doctor about the bad fall he took after a dizzy spell. He recounted the swelling in his ankle, his difficulty walking, and the sometimes excruciating pain that ran from the ball of his foot to his femur.

"We'll do X-rays."

Benjamin suddenly realized that he wouldn't be able to attend Séverin Gaesler's funeral. All the standing up, sitting down, and kneeling during the service, followed by the walking in the cemetery, would be more than he could bear.

"In your opinion, what's wrong with my foot?" Benjamin asked.

"Frankly, dear friend, I'm leaning toward a trauma to the joint. A musculoskeletal injury caused by the stretching or possibly the tearing of ligaments in your ankle. Simply put, I'm betting on a sprain. But again, we need to take X-rays."

Benjamin let out a relieved sigh. "Well, that's a relatively simple thing to treat, isn't it, doctor?"

"Yes, in fact it is. Do you have anyone who can drive you to Colmar for the X-rays? If not, I can take you there after lunch. I'll be done with my patients by then."

"That won't be necessary, doctor. My assistant can do it."

"You'll be fixed up quite easily. You might need a brace and crutches, but if the sprain is mild, ice and rest may do the trick. You'll be back on a good stem in no time. But I do advise you to see your doctor when you get back home. You should try to find out what caused that dizzy spell."

"Thank you, doctor." Benjamin could already feel the color coming back to his cheeks and the tension draining from his neck and shoulders. Although he'd need to go easy on his ankle, the injury didn't appear to be anything serious.

Dr. Cayla, however, wasn't done with him. In fact, he was quite curious. What winds had brought the winemaker to the land of Alsace? What did he think of the most recent vintage that was already being praised? What did he predict for this year's late-harvest wines? The wine expert was happy to answer. He sensed a man with refined taste and a reliable palate. This was someone who most certainly had more than a few good Burgundies in his wine cellar, as well as wines from across the Rhine, probably bottles of Palatinat, Wurttemberg, and Hesse-Rhénanie.

"How fortunate you are to be practicing medicine in the heart of a region that produces the best wines in Alsace."

"I'll drink to that," the old physician joked as he scribbled a prescription for a pain reliever.

"Take the Deutzlers," Benjamin continued. "Now there's a family that fate hasn't spared, and yet they produce impeccable grand crus, like Kirchberg and Osterberg. Speaking of the Deutzlers, I was sorry to hear about Vincent Deutzler, and I just saw Véronique in your waiting room."

"Yes, Véronique is one of my patients," the practitioner said, pushing up his glasses. "That poor girl has been under a cloud of bad luck for some time now."

"In the waiting room she said she was having a flare-up of her carpal tunnel. That's a repetitive-motion injury, isn't it? Estate owners are always telling me about their day laborers with sore arms and wrists. The workers say they can't sleep at night, and their hands and arms are either numb or they tingle."

"Musculoskeletal problems in the world of winemaking aren't something to take lightly, Mr. Cooker. Wrist and hand injuries from vine pruning are common. But workers are at risk of developing other health problems, as well—asthma from exposure to pesticides, for example."

"Asthma—that's something that hadn't occurred to me, Dr. Cayla. But let's get back to the musculoskeletal problems."

"Yes, of course. Thirty percent of these injuries are related to pruning activities, but we're talking about other parts of the body, in addition to the arms and hands. Seven to ten percent of all pruners have shoulder pain. Twelve percent suffer from epicondylitis—"

"From what?" asked Benjamin.

"That would be elbow pain, what some people call tennis elbow. According to some estimates, a quarter of all pruners have chronic pain in the hand or wrist, or both. More than ten percent have nocturnal paresthesias, the pins-and-needles tingling that interferes with sleep. This is a common symptom of carpal tunnel syndrome, which is compression of a nerve in the wrist. Some people don't have any feeling at all in their hands."

"So can surgery alleviate some of the symptoms?"

"Yes, it can. And the surgery is a relatively simple procedure."

"Tell me, Dr. Cayla, when is this type of surgery performed?"

"Usually, surgery is a last resort. First we advise the patient to apply cold packs and take frequent breaks, which isn't always easy if you're working in a vineyard. Sometimes we splint the wrist. If that doesn't work, we often prescribe anti-inflammatory medications. If the symptoms are severe, we advise surgery."

"That's not exactly what I'm trying to get at, Dr. Cayla. When do these repetitive-motion injuries tend to flare up?"

"Oh, I'd say I see most of my carpal-tunnel patients during the pruning season. In the winter, after the first frost. They start coming to see me in January. From then on, my office is never empty."

"Wouldn't you say it's unusual to have a flare-up at this time of year?"

"Unusual, maybe. But not necessarily unlikely. Remember, any kind of activity, especially strenuous or out-of-the-ordinary activity, can exacerbate an existing condition. For example, I wouldn't advise you to take up the violin, Mr. Cooker, if you already had carpal tunnel."

"I can assure you, I won't be taking up the violin, even though my wrist is just fine."

"Tell me, Mr. Cooker, you wouldn't happen to be some kind of detective on the side, would you?"

"You might say that," Benjamin replied, glancing at the mantel of the doctor's small fireplace. It was piled high with medical journals and pharmaceuticals. "Thank you for seeing me on such short notice."

"It was no problem at all." The doctor got up and gave Benjamin the smile that had certainly reassured hundreds of patients over the years. He accompanied the winemaker back to the waiting room and asked him to return the following day with his X-rays.

"Soon the sprain will be just a troublesome memory, Mr. Cooker." The two men parted with a warm and firm handshake.

The café was nearly empty, and Virgile had settled himself on a stool at the zinc counter. From there he had a clear view of the door to the doctor's office across the street and Benjamin's car, which he had parked along the curb. He ordered a coffee and struck up a conversation with the woman running the place. Although her brown hair and slim figure were attractive, she looked like she was forty going on sixty. The bitterness in her eyes aged her considerably.

The conversation inevitably turned to the vineyard destruction, but the woman had nothing new to tell him. As she was speculating on the next targets, a man caught Virgile's eye. He had walked up to the Mercedes, and now he was crouching near the rear wheels.

"I'll be right back he said," Virgile said, jumping up from his stool and rushing toward the car. Virgile recognized André Deutzler. Seeing him coming, André sidled over to his motorcycle— an old-model Yamaha. He put on his helmet, pretending not to recognize Virgile, and straddled his cycle.

Three minutes later a woman wearing a leather jacket and an arm sling walked over and got on the cycle behind him. Virgile was even more shocked when he realized who it was: Véronique Deutzler.

Wondering what that was all about, Virgile returned to the bar.

"Well, surprise, surprise," the woman behind the counter said. "Véronique Deutzler making another visit to the good doctor."

"You know her?"

"Yeah, I know her."

"I understand she's had a rough time of it," Virgile said, hoping to draw out some gossip.

The woman harrumphed and continued wiping down the counter.

"First, the family's vines were destroyed, and then she lost her father-in-law," Virgile said. "It must be tough on her, being pregnant and all. Good thing she's got her husband at her side."

"At her side maybe, but I'm not so sure he's the one in her bed."

"What do you mean by that?"

"Let's just say there is some question about the baby being his."

"My grandfather used to say, 'Infidelity is an itch that it's best not to scratch.' Are you telling me that she scratched the itch?"

The barista smiled. "There've been lots of stories since she married Iselin. He doesn't have much in the looks department, and you couldn't blame a girl for checking a guy out from time to time. But jumping in the sack with your husband's own brother? Now that's something you just don't do. I'll say this for André: he's shy and doesn't have much to say, but he can put in a good day's work."

"And old man Deutzler?" Virgile asked. "Did he know what was going on?"

"He seemed to put up with the whole situation, although it had to grate on him that André was cuckolding his golden boy, Iselin. Actually, I heard Deutzler's nurse was keeping him preoccupied. She was devoted—that one."

"I'm sure he enjoyed his sponge baths," Virgile said. "I'm guessing she threw in a massage every once in a while."

"He threw in something, too, if you get my drift. I heard she made a trip to the hospital in Strasbourg to nip that in the bud. But who knows? Maybe the old bugger had a third son we don't know about."

"What a family," Virgile said. "And what about the child Véronique is carrying? Do you think it is Iselin's or André's?"

"I'd guess André. He's the one she seems to love. As for the other one, he just sits back and plays with his corkscrew."

At that moment, Virgile saw Benjamin on the office doorstep. He paid his bill, thanked the woman, flashed her one of his smiles, and headed across the street.

"We need to go to Colmar. I have to get my foot X-rayed," Benjamin said.

"Boss, I just spared you another incident," Virgile said, as they slowly made their way to the car.

Benjamin lowered himself into the passenger seat. "I'm listening, my guardian angel."

"I was careful to park your car within view of the café. Well, about forty-five minutes later, a guy began to prowl around it. I watched his every move. When he started taking too close a look at the rear tires, I jumped up and scared him off. You know who it was? Guess! You won't believe it."

"The younger Deutzler son," Benjamin replied.

"How did you know?"

"My injury hasn't affected my brain, Virgile."

"Well, then, guess who he took off with."

"His sister-in-law."

Virgile stared at his boss. Even with a bum foot, the winemaker was always one step ahead.

12

Virgile had no interest in waiting while Benjamin had his X-rays done. The bench in the waiting area was hard. The fluorescent lights were harsh, and he had better things to do. With Benjamin's blessings, he decided to pay Inspector Fauchié a visit.

The police station on the Rue du Chasseur was relatively calm. Nobody was waiting around in handcuffs. The green plants in the corridor were perfectly watered, and the female officer behind the reception desk was bent over the horoscopes in the *Dernières Nouvelles d'Alsace*. When Virgile's arrival was announced, the inspector emerged from his office right away. In a gesture of friendship and perhaps affection, Fauchié even put his hand on the young man's shoulder.

"How have you been since yesterday morning, Virgile? And how is Mr. Cooker?"

Fauchié motioned Virgile into his office. Virgile sat down and gave the inspector a brief but comprehensive summary of the previous forty-eight hours. He didn't omit a single detail: the trip to Thierenbach, the winemaker's unfortunate fall, the consultation with Dr. Cayla, the information regarding repetitive-motion injuries, Véronique Deutzler's wrist problems, the scene with the Mercedes convertible, and André's suspicious behavior, including his escape like a bat out of hell on a Yamaha 350, with his sister-in-law clinging to his back.

"A motorcycle, you say?"

"Yes, orange. An old model. Not very classy, but it really hauls ass!"

"I see," Fauchié said, playing with a paperclip.

Virgile was fully enjoying the moment. He had delivered the solution to the mystery on a silver platter. All that was left to do now was trail and then snatch the couple like ripe grapes. Catching them in the act was Roch's job. He alone, along with the public prosecutor, of course, could deal the final blow.

"Unless," suggested the inspector, his gaze lost in the black-and-white photo where he stood beaming with his wife and the young Damien.

"Unless?" Virgile asked.

Watching the way Fauchié was playing with the paperclip, undoing every bend and working out each kink, Virgile could only imagine the strategy the police inspector was silently formulating. The law-enforcement machine was far too complex for Virgile. He didn't even want to think about it.

Hailstones began hitting the windows of the inspector's office. A storm had been threatening for an hour, and the city had been blanketed in a thick veil of dark crepe. Now it had started.

Having been manipulated too much, Fauchié's paperclip finally broke. Fauchié leaned his head against the back of his chair, closed his eyes, and smiled. Virgile thought he saw a trace of mischief—even cunning—on Fauchié's face when he opened his eyes again.

"Virgile, it's my turn to give you some firsthand information, which should please you."

"I'm eager to hear it."

"I've been forcing myself to drink two glasses of Bordeaux at each meal, and I have to admit I derive a certain pleasure from it."

"It's about time," replied Benjamin. Virgile turned around and saw the winemaker standing in the doorway, the blue envelope containing his X-rays peeking out from under his drenched Loden.

Dr. Cayla had been entirely correct. The X-rays confirmed a mild sprain, which would heal nicely as long as Benjamin used a crutch, iced his ankle as often as possible, and put his foot up whenever he could. He had promised the blond technician that he would do just that before taking the large blue envelope and saying good-bye.

"Delighted to see you again, Mr. Cooker," Fauchié said, inviting Benjamin into his office. "Please take a seat. Virgile told me all about your problems. There's no fracture, I hope."

"Just a sprain," the winemaker answered, leaning his crutch against a side table.

"Your timing couldn't be better, in light of the information your assistant has just relayed. It's invaluable. To reach our goal, however, I need what you might call..."

"A bending of official procedure?" Benjamin could read the inspector's mind.

"A bending of procedure?" Virgile said. "I'm not following."

"We're not talking about a bending per se, son," the winemaker said. "It's more of a dislocation involving the two arms of law enforcement. I believe Dr. Cayla would describe a dislocation as the displacement of two articular surfaces that have lost their natural connection. In this case, we're talking about the gendarmerie and the police. They work together most of the time, but their connection isn't compulsory."

"My friend, I see that you understand me completely," said Fauchié.

"To put it plainly, Virgile, the police inspector does not intend to give any new ammunition to Roch. Especially since the little twerp... Pardon me, Inspector Fauchié. I hope you'll excuse the term."

Fauchié chuckled and picked up another paperclip.

"Especially since Roch is already passing himself off to the prefect as the butcher, the baker, and the candlestick maker," Benjamin said.

Virgile got up from his chair and began pacing around Fauchié's desk. The inspector made no objection. He then picked up Benjamin's crutch and pointed it at a large wall map of Alsace, stretching from Strasbourg to Colmar.

Like a general brandishing his baton at the mock-up of a battlefield, Virgile aimed the crutch at Ingersheim, a winemaking village on the edge of Colmar.

Benjamin and the inspector looked at each other, speechless.

"Could you be more explicit, Virgile?" Benjamin asked.

The stormy weather had dissipated, leaving an ashen sky and a barometer pointing to dry cold. Snow had even made an appearance in the Vosges Mountains and would reach the plains and valleys in a matter of hours. The old wine-makers watched the winter weather arrive as they checked their vines and prayed that the maniac with the power tool would spare them.

Benjamin remained cloistered in his room the entire day, putting his tasting notes in order, reflecting on his evaluations of some rather unpromising samples of sparkling wines, and keeping his leg up. He had called Elisabeth to tell her about his accident, and she had made him promise to take care of his ankle.

"Promise or I'll call Virgile," she threatened. "You know what a nag he can be."

"I promise, dear. I'll be almost as good as new by the time I get home. I can't wait to see you."

When the church bells rang, Benjamin had a compassionate thought for Séverin Gaesler, who was being buried in a cemetery plot without many flowers or wreaths. Perhaps there might be some yarrow pulled from the hills near the Koenigsbourg castle. Benjamin also thought of Jeanne and pledged to say a prayer for both her and Vincent Deutzler near the Pillar of Angels before leaving Alsace. He didn't think he had the courage to look at the Grim Reaper in the clock. He'd make it a point not to be there on the hour, when the Reaper banged the bronze bell. He was sure Virgile wouldn't join him. His assistant had already seen the clock, and he'd be more interested in the holiday market stalls on the square.

All day long, Benjamin Cooker was feeling a nostalgia that bordered on depression. He'd put his pen down and look out the window. Then he'd pick it up again and look blankly at his notes. His ankle was hurting, even though he was keeping it up and icing it. "I should have gone back to see Dr. Cayla," Benjamin muttered. "And here I thought I was a hale and hearty English-gent-turned-Frenchman. What a joke that was."

Benjamin realized he had to face facts. Yes, he had many good years ahead of him, but he was getting on and had to pay more attention to his health. And the three deaths he had encountered during his stay in Alsace had certainly delivered the message that he was mortal. He thought about Jean de la Bruyère, who wrote: "Death happens but once, yet we feel it every moment of our lives; it is worse to dread it than to suffer it."

The motorcycle was racing toward them, along the secondary road connecting Colmar's industrial zone and the town of Ingersheim. Wearing bulletproof vests and fluorescent armbands, Inspector Fauchié's men had placed a spike strip across the road. All of the officers were armed with submachine guns. A few yards uphill, a camera mounted on an unmarked car had been activated fifteen seconds earlier.

Coming upon the roadblock, the motorcyclist braked hard and started losing control. He tried to make a U-turn, but two officers on motorcycles and three in a cruiser quickly overtook him. The motorcyclist's last attempt to escape failed. The machine skidded on the asphalt, sending out a shower of sparks before hitting a tree.

When the groggy motorcyclist tried to rise to his feet, two officers pounced on him and cuffed his hands behind his back. As they started to hoist him up, one of the officers shouted to his superior.

"All right, boss, we've got him!"

Inspector Fauchié walked over to the motorcyclist, whose helmet had probably saved him from a fatal head injury. Checking for weapons, he patted the boy's torso and quickly detected something metal. Fauchié ran his hands down the boy's back and around his middle. That was when he found the battery charger, attached to a power pruner by a wire sewn into the liner of his leather jacket.

When Fauchié finally removed the helmet concealing the identity of the vandal who had sown terror across Alsace, the man spit in his face. The inspector responded with an uppercut that transformed André Deutzler's mouth into a mass of Burgundy-colored pulp.

With some parting advice, Dr. Cayla put Benjamin Cooker on the path to recovery. Benjamin didn't mind that he'd still have to use the crutch. He knew he'd be feeling better soon, and the follow-up visit with the doctor was already improving his spirits. It gave him the opportunity to discuss Alsace wines and perhaps catch up on some gossip.

"So tell me, Dr. Cayla, have you heard how Véronique Deutzler's doing?" Benjamin asked.

"Since her father-in-law died, I understand she's gotten a part-time secretarial job at the wine cooperative in Ribeauvillé. She doesn't have to do any more pruning, and she's been able to get out from under her husband's thumb. He's never been the easiest person to live with."

As Benjamin left the doctor's office, he tried to pay the man his well-earned fee. The doctor wouldn't hear of it, so Benjamin promised him some bottles of wine he had just had the pleasure of helping to produce in Germany, along with a bottle of Saint Émilion grand cru classé. Benjamin had recently learned that the property was in the process of changing hands.

Saying a warm good-bye to his new Alsatian friend, the winemaker added, "Don't drink to my health, or else we might never see each other again."

Benjamin sniffed the crisp air and sensed that snow was on its way. He had intentionally parked his convertible on a dead-end street across from the Rue des Tonneliers. From the Café des Sports, he watched the comings and goings of Dr. Cayla's office. He saw Véronique Deutzler go in, her arm still in a sling. When she came out, the winemaker improvised a chance encounter. The young woman backed away and tried to cut short any small talk.

"I need to talk to you, Mrs. Deutzler."

"I have nothing to say to you."

"Maybe not to me. But you do owe the police an explanation."

"What are you trying to say?"

Benjamin simply looked at the wrist in a sling.

"It's cold out here. Let's go have a cup of coffee. What do you say?"

Véronique looked down and didn't say anything. Finally, she nodded and let Benjamin lead her to the café. They seated themselves at the back, on garnet-colored benches, facing each other across a table. All around, posters advertised various brews: Lutèce, Abbaye de Leffe, Affligem, and Amstel.

"How is André doing?" Benjamin asked.

"I don't know. None of us have been approved for visitation yet. His lawyer says we have to be patient."

"Has he finally confessed?" asked Benjamin.

"Yes," the young woman answered. She hadn't touched her coffee.

"Has he told them everything?"

"I don't know…"

"He's protecting you, isn't he?"

Benjamin looked closely now at the woman who was finally, awkwardly, bringing the cold cup of coffee to her lips. Her hands were shaking, and there was something otherworldly in her gaze.

"I have nothing to do with this business…"

"No, you're not responsible for your brother-in-law's mental illness—a brother-in-law who, I believe, is also your lover. On the other hand, you became an accomplice to the acts for which he is in jail today. And it would be useless to deny it."

The young woman, whose back was to the rest of the room, burst into tears.

"You helped him when there were two attacks several miles apart. You even ended up hurting yourself. He never showed you how to use those power shears, did he? And you already had carpal tunnel syndrome."

Véronique Deutzler, her eyes still teary, stared at one of the posters on the wall.

"It wasn't my idea. It was André's. He became completely absorbed in what he was doing. Every morning he'd run out to buy the papers so he could read what they were writing about him. He reveled in being the most-wanted man in Alsace. He thought he was indomitable."

As she confided in Benjamin, Véronique slipped her wedding ring off her finger and put it on again.

"I never loved Iselin. I was still living in my parents' home, with no prospects. Then Iselin showed up, and for the first time I saw a future for myself. That didn't last long. He wasn't a good husband. I wound up falling in love with André, who wasn't anything like his brother. I even dreamed of having a baby with him."

"And so you just gave up on Iselin?"

"Yeah, you could say that. He has just one love: his wine. The only thing he wants me for is making his supper at night. And his arrogance is insufferable. He's his daddy's boy, and he knows it. He was sick for three months the year you gave him a bad rating. He hated you for doing that. And guess who slashed the tires on your fancy Mercedes? It was Iselin."

The winemaker didn't react. He simply went from one question to the next.

"And why did André vandalize the Ginsmeyers' vines in Ammerschwihr?"

"To get even with Laetitia, the Ginsmeyer daughter who snubbed him in ninth grade."

"Your André knows how to hold a grudge, doesn't he?"

"He's not a bad person, Mr. Cooker. It's just that he's been hurt. And he remembers each one of his hurts, from the day his mother committed suicide. How different things would have been if she had lived. He just wanted to even the score. He thought it would make him feel better. I told him it was no way to deal with his pain. I told him he'd wind up getting arrested, but he wouldn't listen."

"From there to destroying his own vines, now that's a big leap. Unless it was to quell suspicions," Benjamin said, looking into the bottom of his cup, where the traces of coffee grounds remained.

"That's easy to explain. The night before, the old man had drawn up a new will. He was planning to give all the young vines, plus the best parcels of Osterberg, to Iselin. André was getting

161

his least-productive vineyards, and he was furious. He wanted to kill the old man, who was already talking about marrying that bitch of a nurse who was wagging her tongue all over the place about André and me."

"You don't have her to worry about her anymore, do you? She's in jail too. The medical examiners found fibers in your father-in-law's nose. The fibers were from the pillow she used to smother him."

"Like I said, she was a bitch. She didn't like the will either. She and the old man had a son nobody knew about, and Vincent made no provisions for him in the will. Yeah, those two—the old man and the nurse—were a real piece of work."

Benjamin couldn't help thinking about the nurse's limp. Bitch or witch doing the devil's bidding—which was she? Maybe both.

"Getting back to André, why did he go on to vandalize the Klipsherrers, the Flancks, and all the others?"

"It was them or someone else. It didn't matter. André was too crazy by that time. He said he had to make the vines bleed every night. It was an addiction. And he was getting more reckless. I knew it would end with him in handcuffs."

Véronique's lichen-colored eyes reminded Benjamin of the moss on dead trees. She had stopped crying, but her face was pale, and her hands were still shaking.

"Are you all right, Mrs. Deutzler?"

"It's just the stress of everything. It's gotten to me. I can't stop shaking."

"A little Alsatian cognac might help you feel better," Benjamin suggested, putting his hand on Véronique's wrist.

"Probably it would, but just order one for yourself. I'll take some water." Véronique was staring out the window, where snowflakes were softly falling.

A shimmering shroud of snow covered the Rue des Tonneliers. Ribeauvillé had reclaimed its purity.

EPILOGUE

Charming wooden cottages, all of them hastily constructed and given over to holiday commercialism, are everywhere, offering the merchandise of master glassmakers, cabinet makers, liquorists, wood carvers, milliners, jewelers, confectioners, butchers, and beekeepers. Above these makeshift structures, garlands of holiday lights add to the fairyland ambiance that delights both children and young-at-heart adults.

In this resplendent souk appealing to the eye and tickling the nose, a woman threads her way to the Strasbourg cathedral. Her long black coat is sprinkled with snow, as is her curly hair, which peeks out from a thick woolen cap.

Her pace is urgent, and her eyes seem reddened from the cold. She lowers her head as if to avoid the delighted faces of children hanging onto their mothers' hands. This overwhelming feast, with its lacquered toys and smells of licorice and honey nauseates her. She heads for the entrance to the cathedral, and without even looking at the tympanum, she enters the massive space.

Obviously, a Mass has just ended. Two acolytes in white vestments are cleaning the side table and extinguishing the candles. In the chapel of the Blessed Virgin, a woman is arranging Christmas roses in a huge vase. When she bends down to collect a few stems that have fallen to the floor, the old woman reveals her swollen ankles and the pale flesh of her calves. She's quietly chanting a prayer.

The woman in black is much younger than her somber coat suggests. She plunges her fingers into the holy water and makes the sign of the cross. She slips into a pew in the back and kneels for a moment. Then she quickly stands again. The baby's movements in her womb are too strong. She covers her face with her clasped hands, but doesn't pray. Tears are rolling down her cheeks, still rosy from the cold. She doesn't hear the tourists who, under the tutelage of their guide, are gathered in front of the monumental clock.

The woman learned this morning that her unborn child will never know his father. The previous night, André Deutzler slit his wrists in his prison cell in Oermingen. His cellmate, a young Madagascan with cauliflower ears, heard nothing and discovered him at dawn, lying in a pool of blood.

The visitors are hanging onto the words of the young guide, who's reciting a memorized presentation. He's talking about angels, the four seasons, calendars, movable feasts, apparent solar time and mean solar time, Mars, Jupiter, and Saturn, the lunar globe, Copernicus and Galileo...

The Grim Reaper interrupts the guide. He strikes the bell with his ivory femur. It's noon.

The Schwilgué clock's parade of apostles can now begin. As the tourists marvel at the sight, Véronique begins to sob. She has made up her mind: she will never return to Ribeauvillé. At two o'clock she will take the train to Germany and carry with her nothing but this new life in her womb.

Thank you for reading Late Harvest Havoc.

We invite you to share your thoughts and reactions on your favorite social media and retail platforms.

We appreciate your support.

The Winemaker Detective Series

An epicurean immersion in French countryside and gourmet attitude with two expert winemakers turned amateur sleuths gumshoeing around wine country. The following titles are available in English.

Treachery in Bordeaux
Barrels at the prestigious grand cru Moniales Haut-Brion wine estate in Bordeaux have been contaminated. Is it negligence or sabotage?
www.treacheryinbordeaux.com

Grand Cru Heist
Benjamin Cooker retreats to the region around Tours to recover from a carjacking and turns PI to solve two murders and a very particular heist. Who stole those bottles of grand cru classé?
www.grandcruheist.com

Nightmare in Burgundy
The winemaker detective leaves his native Bordeaux for a dream wine tasting trip to Burgundy that turns into a troubling nightmare.
www.nightmareinburgundy.com

Deadly Tasting

A serial killer stalks Bordeaux. To understand the wine-related symbolism, the local police call on the famous wine critic Benjamin Cooker.

www.deadlytasting.com

Cognac Conspiracies

The heirs to one of the oldest Cognac estates in France face a hostile takeover by foreign investors. In what he thought was a sleepy provincial town, Benjamin Cooker and his assistant Virgile have their loyalties tested.

www.cognacconspiracies.com

Mayhem in Margaux

Benjamin Cooker is focused on solving a mystery that touches him very personally. Along the way he finds out more than he'd like to know about the makings of a grand cru classé wine.

www.mayheminmargaux.com

Flambé in Armagnac

The Winemaker Detective heads to Gascony, where a fire has ravaged the warehouse of one of the region's finest Armagnac producers, and a small town holds fiercely onto its secrets.

www.flambeinarmagnac.com

Montmartre Mysteries
The Winemaker Detective visits a favorite wine shop in Paris and stumbles upon an attempted murder, drawing him into investigation that leads them from the Foreign Legion to the Côte du Rhône.

www.montmartremysteries.com

Backstabbing in Beaujolais
Can the Winemaker Detective and his assistant keep calculating real estate agents, taciturn winegrowers, dubious wine merchants and suspicious deaths from delaying delivery of the world-famous Beaujolais Nouveau?

www.backstabbinginbeaujolais.com

ABOUT THE AUTHORS

Noël Balen (left) and Jean-Pierre Alaux (right).
(©David Nakache)

Jean-Pierre Alaux and **Noël Balen** came up with the winemaker detective over a glass of wine, of course. Jean-Pierre Alaux is a magazine, radio, and television journalist when he is not writing novels in southwestern France. The grandson of a winemaker, he has a real passion for food, wine, and winemaking. For him, there is no greater common denominator than wine. Coauthor of the series Noël Balen lives in Paris, where he writes, makes records, and lectures on music. He plays bass, is a music critic, and has authored a number of books about musicians, in addition to many novels and short stories.

ABOUT THE TRANSLATOR

Sally Pane studied French at State University of New York Oswego and the Sorbonne before receiving her Masters Degree in French Literature from the University of Colorado. Her career includes more than twenty years of translating and teaching French and Italian, and she has translated a number of titles in the Winemaker Detective series. She lives in Boulder, Colorado, with her husband.

DISCOVER MORE BOOKS FROM

LE FRENCH BOOK
www.lefrenchbook.com

White Leopard
by Laurent Guillaume

Shadow Ritual
by Eric Giacometti and Jacques Ravenne

The Collector
by Anne-Laure Thiéblemont

**The Paris Homicide series
by Frédérique Molay**

The Paris Lawyer
by Sylvie Granotier

The Greenland Breach
by Bernard Besson

**The Consortium thrillers
by David Khara**

CPSIA information can be obtained at www.ICGtesting.com
Printed in the USA
LVOW06s1605091215

466130LV00001B/43/P